The Strange Fruits of
Sarah Bartman

By Julius Kane

Maverick Media Group

The Strange Fruits of Sarah Bartman by Julius Kane

If you purchase this book without a cover you should be aware that this book may have been stolen property and reported as unsold and destroyed to the publisher. In such case neither the author nor the publisher has received any payment for this "stripped book."

This book is a work of fiction. Names, characters, places and incidents were created from the imagination of its writer and are used fictitiously. Any similarities between actual events or persons living or dead are coincidental.

Copyright © 2016

All Rights Reserved. No part of this publication may be reproduced or transmitted an any form or by any means, electronic or mechanical, including photocopy, recording or any information storage and retrieval system, without permission in writing from the publisher.

Requests for permission to make copies or perform any part of this work should be sent to: juliuskane@ymail.com

ISBN: 978-0-9785056-9-1

Cover Design: Julius Kane
Cover Photo: Amara Shukur

For my family. I love you all!

<u>Characters</u>

Sarah
Doctor
Mother
Bakari
Nateeya
George
Activist
Constable Lahey
1st Woman
Prostitute
2nd Woman
Stranger
Drummer Boy
Shepherd
Researcher
Wife
Husband
Judge
Culvier
Child

[Center Stage.]

Doctor.   I know you. And I know you. You have come here tonight to judge me. To point your fingers and say "he's a bad man." Although I lived over 200 years ago, has the world really changed? I see improvements in science, medicine, and education. You're even sending men into outer space. But you cannot seem to fix your social structures. That should be easier then walking on mars.

Now, I've only been to America twice and I actually enjoyed it. The cities were hubs of activity. However, you all seemed divided on one very important issue: *The all men are created equal dilemma.* Half of you believe that to be true, while the other half who do not, fight and kill those that do. You call America home of the free but there are more people in prison here then anywhere else in the world. And you know who put them in prison? All of you who proclaim all men are created equal. Well, I am absolutely perplexed. How can you point your self righteous fingers at me when there are three fingers pointing back at you?

[Open Curtain.]

Act 1

(Scene: The year is 1810; a seaside village in South Africa. An African family is outside washing clothes and preparing food.)

Bakari. Behold the size of my bounty. They say the mudfish are very hard to catch. And I caught four. That means I'm the best fisherman in the entire village. **(Beats chest)** Wait until ma-ma sees this.

Sarah. You are crazy. But you will make a great mate to your new wife. You are so happy when you make a big catch.

Bakari. (Bear hugs Sarah) Why shouldn't I be?

Sarah. Put me down strong man. You are ready for the wrestling tournament.

Bakari. The elders don't think so. But they'll see. By next season, I will be fit.

Sarah. Yesterday, you boasted being the best hunter in the entire village. You want to do it all.

Bakari. Yes, and today I became the best

fisherman. See, you can tell they're full grown by the markings on the tail. This is a big week. God is pleased. I've been practicing my throw and thrust. I shall kill a lion tomorrow.

Sarah. A lion you say?

Bakari. Have you forgotten? Tomorrow starts the big hunt. All the young males are sharpening their spears, speaking their rituals and painting their faces. I will be out front, hunting bravely; as father before me. It is the right of passage.

Sarah. I know. But I still worry about you.

Bakari. It is in the woman's nature to worry. And it is in the man's nature to tell her there is nothing to worry about. The hunt is tradition. It is danger. It is conquering fear. Dada was younger than me when he went on his first, big hunt. I am older than he.

Sarah. And you are not afraid?

Bakari. No, am I not on the doorstep of manhood? I am eager. The ancestors whisper to me. They say, this is the spear that will bring home my prize.

Sarah. You are a man. And I am happy to call you my brother.

Bakari. Sar jai, remember, courage lies in the heart of all Africans and we must make our ancestors proud.

Sarah. Well said brother. I know Dada would be proud of you.

Bakari. Yes. His spirit is around me. I will not let him down. I will not let any of you down.

Sarah. Take this. **(Places beads around his neck)** I made this for you. Me and Nateeya performed a ritual of protection on them. It will bring you good fortune. You will be favored by God.

Bakari. It is beautiful my sister. I will cherish it always. Now, I must go ready myself; prepare and practice. **(Exit.)**

[Enter mother and Nateeya]

Mother. Sar jai.

Sarah. Yes, Ma-ma.

Mother. Ya listen at me good. Ya be me oldest and ya suspose ta be me wisest. These be ya fruits girl. **(Points to her body)** Ya cain't let nubody touch and taste da fruits from ya tree. Lest him be ya mate.

Sarah. I have not.

Mother. Me see ya and Agu holding hands. And him be tryin' to get cha alone. And what me be tellin' ya?

Sarah. He took my hand and that was all. You said to bring Nateeya with me and I did. But he was just taking me to see the missionaries.

Mother. That's what he say. But dere be a lot of stops along the way. So ya take ya sista and ya brotha too. **(Pause)** Missionaries! Dey come and tell ya to talk English like dem and den pray ta Jesus like dem do. Me hear people close dey eye ta pray and dey get bumped in dey head.

Nateeya. Yeah, and some of them have not been seen again. Even the elders say as much.

Sarah. Well, they won't get me.

Nateeya. Why not?

Sarah. Because I hits hard! **(She pretends to hit Nateeya and they tussle about)**

Mother. Ya two stop ya foolishness. We need to... **(Places hand to head)**

Sarah. What's wrong ma-ma?

Nateeya. Another hot spell. Get her some water.

Sarah. That's the second time this week. We must take her to see the medicine man or to the missionaries.

Mother. Hush now, stop ya fussin'. Me not go

nowhere near dem missionaries; strange devils with new medicine.

Sarah. Ma-ma, times are changing. The new medicine can work better than the old medicine; faster too.

Mother. Me no trust dem. Make my special tea. And put dem herbs and spices in it. Once de work git done, we can take a long rest. Me be okay. Yeah, it will pass. Be... alright.

Nateeya. Ma-ma, please rest a bit. **(Helps mother sit down.)**

Sarah. Ma-ma is more stubborn than that ox.

Nateeya. Dada was the same way before he died. Just beat.

Sarah. He worked himself to death.

Nateeya. The priestess said the river basin was poisoned.

Sarah. Maybe, but dada worked sun up to sun down.

Nateeya. It was not for nothing. If we work this land for 15 more years it be ours.

Sarah. Ma-ma cannot do this for fifth- teen more years. That is why I will start trading goods at the

Seaport...and in the marketplace...and with the missionaries too.

Nateeya.   What will you sell and trade?

Sarah. I will make hundreds...no thousands of these beads and earrings to match. And I will paint them so many colors that when the people get off the ships from around the world, they will want one. I will sell ointments and oils. Hand crafted oil burners.

Nateeya. Oh, they are so beautiful; polished and strong.

Sarah. You can help me by gathering materials and finding shells and painting them. You thought I would leave you out?

Nateeya. What about Bakari? He is a good craftsman.

Sarah. He can help too. It will be a family company.

Nateeya. Oh Sar jai, do you really think we can make a lot of money?

Sarah. Yes we can. I will teach Bakari and you everything mother taught me about making crafts. We will bring in a months wages in a matter of days. We will make so much money ma-ma will not have to ever work again. Come, I will show you how easy they are to make. **(Exit)**

[Enter Doctor, Captain and Shepherd]

Captain. Doctor Dunlap, must you always near about at every port?

Doctor. My dear captain, I do not merely leer about. I study, I... I observe. I analyze and document important scientific theories. Of course, I don't expect a man who spent half a century rocking back and forth on rusty metal barges just to understand anything as complex as scientific theories.

Captain. What?

Doctor. Perhaps the salt water has not only corroded your ship but your cerebrum as well.

Captain. Was that your idea of an insult, doctor? Because I'll leave you your baggage, your man servant and your scientific theories right here on the damn loading dock. Let you study some of this African heat. Now, I need not remind you of the two pounds you are still short on your passage. Then there's that money you owe to some of my men on those stupid wages you lost. And believe me, they're anxious to collect.

Doctor. I assure you captain, as soon as we reach London Harbor, all debts will be paid forth right.

Captain. They better be. And you sir need to be

back on board by 0600 hours. **(Exits)**

Doctor. Come along shepherd.

Shepherd. Yes sir.

Doctor. This heat is simply dreadful. But it doesn't seem to bother you a bit, Shepard. You're tough, dark flash provides the perfect camouflage against those cursed sun rays, while my tender white skin seems to burn most excessively. It's exactly the way God, in his infinite wisdom, and Mother Nature, as it were, designed us to be. It is abundantly clear; we are the Sayers and ye are the doers. Whites are made to be indoors, thinking and planning. And blacks were meant to be outdoors, toiling and laboring. I must write that down immediately. Shepherd, give me my fountain and ink.

Shepherd. Yes, sir.

Doctor. Let's see, where was I? Oh yes; superior by design. We are the brains and they are the bronze, the beauty to their beast, and the light to their darkness. In more elementary terms; the quintessential white collar worker to the blue collar worker. Now, this simply reverts back to that brilliant thesis I wrote about the white woman's flawless physique compared to the unusual and often distorted bodies of African women. The ladder, of course created for sex and occasional heavy lifting. Shepherd, fetch me a cool drink of water from those Africans over there.

Shepherd. My master is in need of water. Do you have some to spare?

Sarah. Yes. Here.

Doctor. Good lord Shepherd, the features on that African woman are astonishing. I've never seen anything like it. Her breasts are thrice the size of the white women back home. And look at her buttocks. My God...boy! It doesn't even look real. She must have an absolutely insatiable, sexual appetite. The young, African males may very well consider her their Venus, unless of course, there are others like her; which I doubt. Ordinarily, I'd conclude that such a body type was the result of some type of birth defect. However, the natives around here share similar physical characteristics. Although no where near as defined as hers. She has the biggest bottom I have ever seen. And I bet few outsiders have seen such a thing for that matter. **(To Sarah)** Young woman, I say, young woman! What is your name?

Sarah. Me?

Doctor. Yes

Sarah. Um, Sar jai, sir.

Doctor. Well Sar jai, my name is William Dunlap. I am a surgeon aboard that wretched ship docked in your harbor.

Mother. Sir, did me Sar jai do somethn' wrong?

Doctor. On the contrary. I was merely admiring your daughter's unique body. In all my travels I've never seen anything like her; fascinating.

Mother. Her body, sir?

Doctor. Although you all have similar frames, she has a uniquely shaped lower torso amongst other fascinating attributes. I will document such a rare find in my journal. I'd like to ask you a few questions. I'll gladly pay you for your time. Here you are! **(Gives Sarah money)** Now, how old are you?

Sarah. Seventeen, sir.

Doctor. How long have you lived in this village?

Sarah. Always

Doctor. Rest easy, young maiden. You act as if I'm here to drag you off to the local magistrate. I mean you no harm.

Mother. Sir, what more you be wantin'?

Doctor. Well...are you married?

Mother. (Steps in front of Sarah) Me Sar jai promised to de Elder's young son, Trabul. He be of good spirit, too.

Doctor. I see. Are there any other women like you here, Sar jai?

Sarah. Lots and lots of them.

Doctor. I sincerely doubt that. And what do you eat?

Mother. (Interrupts) food...mista.

Sarah. We grow most of our own food here. Peas, wheat, fruit, fish.

Doctor. Where do you draw your water?

Mother. A well, sir. We drink wata from da well.

Doctor. Yes **(steps back)** I was merely trying to ascertain whether contaminants in the drinking water could possibly play a part in such an unusual body structure.

Mother. We go now!

Doctor. Yes, yes of course.

Mother. You and Nateeya finish yu werk. And git more straw.

Doctor. Um...good day. Shepherd, fetch more water.

Shepherd. Yes, sir.

Doctor. Hegel's Theory about natives in hotter climates being inferior is only partially correct. These Africans are also physically inferior to the white race. Of course that also includes the yellow skinned people of the Far East. Most of them are hardly taller than those Pigmies I encountered last month. **(Sips water)** And those colonists in America, although they're white, it's unlikely they can have an intellectual conversation with a school boy; let alone with me. And their American wenches leave much to be desired. At least the Negro woman's body is made to be ravaged.

Even that maniacal blow hard Napoleon knows that a full blooded Englishman was sent here by God to rule all other races. However, if you were to take an animal out of its climate, detach it from its surroundings and unproductive influences, you can teach it anything that you see fit. And it will learn.

 Look at you, Shepherd. When I purchased you from that buffoon of a master in the Americas, you were retarded and underweight. They said you were incapable of learning. Your mother couldn't get you to set the table properly nor work in your master's fields. Although I can understand the latter; picking cotton is ghastly work. But look what I did. I've fattened you up and given you the wardrobe of a gentlemen. You even posses the education of a seventh grade English boy. Why, I'm even considering furthering your basic arithmetic skills next month. Would you like that shepherd?

Shepherd. Yes sir.

Doctor. It has been quite a few years now, has it not Shepherd? Best years of your life; with more to come.

Shepherd. Yes sir Master Dunlap, sir.

Doctor. Do you recall your former master forcing you to lay down in mud puddles and stepping on you to avoid getting his feet wet?

Shepherd. Yes, sir.

Doctor. But I saw the potential in you. And I created a whole new Negro. The domesticated, educated Negro. I shall pat myself on the back for that. What do you think, Shepherd?

Shepherd. Thank you, sir. Could you teach me more about counting coins and their value?

Doctor. (Scoffs) Whatever for?

Shepherd. I'd like to learn more about those equations, multiply and word problems like; when a horse leaves the stable at 3 o'clock and a horse....

Doctor. Quiet, I'm thinking. **(Pause)** well, we best be getting back. It's a pity all of Britain cannot see this Hottentot women's personification of Africa. The former black slaves in England are so few and have become desperately assimilated and domesticated-they're hardly recognized as Africans. The great, white race often forgets God's pecking order; His natural selection. Our own advanced minds and bodies have become intertwined with the impure, uncivilized and downtrodden lesser races.

I'm certain they would be very interested in gazing upon such a sight as that Sar jai; especially the scientific community. She would most certainly get their investigative juices flowing. In fact, I'd wager they'd pay to see something this fascinating. My God, that's it Shepherd. **(Turns to him)** You would pay to see that woman over there wouldn't you? I mean, if you had money that is.

Shepherd. Pay. I don't know what....

Doctor. Quiet, I'm thinking. Why of course you would. Anyone would, if she is displayed properly. Shepherd, I just had an epiphany. I shall take her back to London with us.

Shepherd. Excuse me, sir, that young woman over there? **(Points in wonder)**

Doctor. I'll turn the intellectual community on its ear with such a find. And make a handsome profit to boot. I'll be the toast of London.

Shepherd. I don't think she wants to go to London, sir.

Doctor. What she wants is inconsequential. It's what England needs. It's what Europe needs. And I intend to give it to them. Come along. Stay close. The mother has an inquisitive nature. She'll be less suspicious with another Negro around. But keep your mouth shut. **(To Sarah)** Excuse me. **(Tips hat)**

Mother. Him again!

Doctor. My eyes can't seem to satisfy their curiosity.

Sarah. You want more water?

Mother. Is not the wata he be wantin'.

Doctor. No. Actually I've come with an intriging proposition.

Mother. We don't want nothin' you be sellin'.

Doctor. (Ignores mother) How would you like to own this very land upon which you till? Even that house... your own fields of crop... goats and chickens?

Mother. Mista, you talkin' crazy. He's got that sickness for sure.

Doctor. I assure you that I am in perfect health. Allow me to explain. If this young woman travels back to London with me, I will pay her, you Sarah, ten shillings a week to help me conduct scientific experiments and be a feature in my traveling show.

Sarah. Really! Ten shillings?

Doctor. That is correct. Within a year's time, you shall be able to buy your mother and your sister whatever you please. You no longer have to churn butter or bind wheat for the land owner. In fact, you can purchase land for yourselves around here.

Nateeya. What will she be doing?

Doctor. She will be dressed in your tribal attire and illuminated with precious gemstones. We will travel throughout England demonstrating to Europeans what an African woman looks like in her natural beauty and native customs. Most of those stupid Europeans have never seen an African woman; least not one with such distinctive features as yours. I currently employ several other women from all over the world. We travel about performing their tribal dances and educating people about their customs. It's social science at its best. Shepherd here, is part of the show. And we've been searching for new talent. Aren't we Shepherd?

Shepherd. (Lowers head)

Mother. Why you want me Sar jai?

Doctor. Well, she has that...that, um, unique bone and body structure I spoke of earlier. She would look simply ravishing in a luxurious gown, walking, teaching, and talking to the white citizens of London about your tribal rituals; what you eat and your various medicines. I'll also be explaining how your men hunt with their spears and your governing practices.

Mother. Where she be sleepin'? How will she eat?

Doctor. With me. I'll assume complete responsibility of course.

Mother. You? Me no think ...

Doctor. And my beautiful wife, Agnes. As a matter of fact, she watches and protects all the girls. She deposits their money into savings accounts. She oversees they're eating...and studying... church attendance. We've been married for sixteen glorious years.

Mother. What 'bout dem men who come callin'?

Doctor. They'll be none of that. My wife Agnes is a strict disciplinarian. Her oversight is beyond compare. I assure you she will return home exactly the way she left.

Nateeya. What's London like?

Doctor. I am absolutely giddy that you asked me that. London is the crown of Europe. The water in that container. The biggest brightest city in the world. The people in London never sleep because there's so much going on.

Sarah. They never sleep?

Doctor. Heavens no. There are parties and dancing

and festivities and singing. And the buildings are the size of a hundred of your homes. With the finest brick and mortar money can buy. There are drinking contests and swimming contests. (Smiles at Sarah) You can swim can't you? You're probably the fastest swimmer around here?

Sarah. I love to swim. Ma-ma did you hear that?

Mother. Ya be swimmin' fine in that big ocean ova dere.

Doctor. Did I tell you my beautiful wife was also a teacher? That's right. She teaches the girls reading, writing, and arithmetic. A first-rate education if you ask me. You know how to write don't you?

Doctor. Don't worry you'll learn. And each month, I should make sure every ship that anchors in that harbor has a letter from your Sar jai; hand delivered by a reliable carrier.

Mother. Me Sar jai not go nowhere witcha mista.

Sarah.. No, wait ma-ma. I need to think about this.

Mother. Whatcha mean, think child?

Sarah. I'm a woman now ma-ma. I know my own mind. And we need the money.

Doctor. This is a splendid opportunity for you young Miss. Once in lifetime. Think about it.

Mother. You leave us be mista.

(Ships whistle blows)

Sarah. Can you give us time alone? We must talk about it.

Doctor. Of course. However, you heard that whistle. That ship leaves in half an hour. And it goes without saying; I shall pay for your passage and provide all meals aboard the ship. **(He walks away)**

Mother. Have ya gone crazy child?

Sarah. I want to go see England and make lots of money. I'll come back home with plenty for all of us.

Nateeya. Can I go, too?

Sarah You're only 13. I'm nearly sixteen.

Nateeya. So?

Mother. Ya not go nowhere wit dat wicked, wicked man. This be ya home right here. Ya can't go trouncin' off to some strange land. What if somethin' happen to ya?

Sarah. Nothing's going to happen. This is a new age. A new century. A new beginning. When good things come, we must grab it.

Mother. Dere be nutin' good 'bout that...doctor.

Sarah. You were younger then me when you left your mother and father. You took a chance. That's all I want to do, ma-ma. You and father taught me to be strong and unafraid. And I am not Afraid.

Mother. Don't cha talk 'bout ya fatha. Him not hea to speak. Ya fatha would stand right along wit me. I speak fa him. One mouth, two voices.

Sarah. But he is here ma-ma. I always feel him. His strength is in here. **(Touches her heart)**

Mother. Dis be happenin' too fast. No more talk.

Sarah. But ma-ma.

Mother. No more talk I say. Nobody go wit dat man nowhere. You and ya sista- go home. Go I say. His spirit is no good.

Sarah. But ma-ma. **(Mother gives a stern look while pointing. Sarah and Nateeya exit)**

Doctor. That mother is a problem. She's literally standing in my way. Shepherd, hurry back to the ship and fetch George Nelson.

Shepherd. Maybe she should not....

Doctor. Shut up and do as I say.

Shepherd. Yes... sir **(exits)**

Doctor. (Yells off stage) And tell him I have money.

Nateeya. What are you doing?

Sarah. I'm leaving **(gathering her belongings and putting them into a satchel)**

Nateeya. You heard what ma-ma said. And what about Shaba? You are promised to be his wife.

Sarah. I will return in one year's time.

Nateeya. What about Bakari? Are you not going to say goodbye?

Sarah. That ship is not going to wait. He will only try to stop me.

Nateeya. Why are you doing this? Are you not happy here with us?

Sarah. Yes. I love you. I love the land. It is my home. But I want more for us. I will come back with enough money to buy everything we want and always dreamed about. We can build our own house. On our own land. Buy our own chickens and goats. We can get tables at the market and sell our own crops. And ma-ma won't ever get sick because she will sit back and not have to work anymore. We will get a real doctor. It will be wonderful. Oh sister, I want to see what is beyond the sea. I want to visit other lands. My stomach tingles just thinking about such adventure. Kiss ma-ma and tell her not to worry. Tell Bakari not to be angry and I'll be back before the next festival.

Nateeya. What about me? What will I do without my big sister?

Sarah. Oh... Nateeya You get started making the necklaces and earrings and bracelets; as I taught you. Study the ways of the trade smiths and craftsman. The younger merchants to the south have shown us the way. Soon, you will be ready to swap and barter with the best of them.

(Sarah with her belongings tries to exit but Nateeya grabs her arm)

Nateeya. Sister, are you sure about this?

Sarah. I will see you soon, little one. **(Long hug) (Crosses stage)** Doctor, I'm going. I'm going to London! **(Excited)**

Doctor. Excellent! Excellent! I was just about to come find you. Now, before we depart, there is a small matter of legality we must attend to.

Sarah. Legality?

Doctor. Yes, I have a contract right here. I'm obligated to make sure everything is 100% professional. Sign at the bottom of this paper. You can write your name, can't you?

Sarah. Yes sir. But this paper has no words on it.

Doctor. Not to worry. I'll fill in the particulars later. It's just to make sure you don't run off and seek employment elsewhere. You know, work for someone else after I brought you to London.

Sarah. I would not do that, sir.

Doctor. Let me help you with your belongings. You are going to have a wonderful trip.

Sarah. Where will I be sleeping in England doctor?

Doctor. I have a large estate. You shall have my daughter's room; still decorated with pictures and artwork from her wonderful imagination.

Sarah. Oh, that sounds good.

Doctor. It needs a little light cleaning. It hasn't been occupied in quite some time. My daughter left the nest many years ago; like you're doing now. She's doing quite well too, living in France, unfortunately. I received a letter from her and her mother before we set sail. They seem to like France. I myself never found much use for the French.

(Enter Shepherd and George)

George. Alright, Dunlap, what do you want now? The captain's ready to shove off.

Doctor. Good day George. This is Sar jai. Sar jai

please excuse us. **(Walks out of ear distance)**

George. You brought me all the way down here to meet another one of your wenches?

Doctor. Take a look at her. She's not like anything you've ever seen.

George. I've seen them all. My uncle was an overseer at one of the biggest plantations you've ever seen. This time you've got a dark wench that's built like a stallion. So what?

Doctor. You poor man. You do lack imagination, don't you? At any rate, I have a matter that requires your complete desecration. Are you still able to smuggle contraband on board the ship; without the men alerting the captain?

George. Well, I do so love contraband. As for the men, none of them have the balls to cross me. What have you got?

Doctor. (Looks over in Sarah's direction) I'd like to put her in your cabin.

George. Are you mad? You know how the captain feels about women on board his vessel. And they're hanging slave ship captains from the gallows you know. First, your man servant, now this.

Doctor. I assure you, all of Shepherd's papers are in order.

George. And furthermore, my last stowaway ate more of my rations then I did. I lost near 30 pounds that voyage. You think I don't know that you're at the top of the captain's hurt list?

Doctor. That man is a buffoon. And there are hundreds of ships that would pay handsomely for my services. Listen, I'll take care of her food. But my cabin is always busy. Sea dogs in and out; constantly nagging me for advice- needing help. I don't want prying eyes. This shall be our secret.

Sarah. Doctor, excuse me, sir. Did you say your wife was in France?

Doctor. Yes, that greedy harlot.

Sarah. But you told my mother she was a teacher and that she takes care of the women in your show.

Doctor. Excuse me one moment Sarah. Shepherd; take her things to the ship.

Shepherd. Yes sir. **(Exits)**

Doctor. I made him leave because I don't want him privy to our transaction. Here, this is for you, **(Gives him money)**

George. I knew you'd been holding out.

Sarah. Doctor, your wife isn't a teacher is she?

Doctor. (Looks back at Sarah then gives George

more money)

George. You're quite generous. But what's all this about? Never figured you for the kind who goes all in for a piece of tail; least of all dark meat.

Sarah. Doctor, I don't think you've been telling the truth. I'm not going anywhere with you.

Doctor. Grab her?

George. What?

Doctor. Grab her or return my money.

George. (Bends Sarah's arm behind her back and places his forearm under her neck) Quit your squirming.

Doctor. Good. I'm going to distract the captain and you take her directly to your cabin.

Sarah. Let me go. **(Yells and struggles)** Let me go. Bakari...Ma-ma.... Nateeya...

George. Your kind is strong, and feisty, too. I like that. I like it when they struggle. **(Sniffs)** That young, fresh from the vineyard smell; plucked ripe from mother's nipple. Doctor, I don't think I can guarantee her safety.

Doctor. Her safety? From whom?

George. From me.

(They all exit)

(Enter Mother and Bakari)

Bakari. This is the finest shield and spear I have ever made. I also have arrows with metal tips dipped in the hot flames of Methu Valley. Wait until Sar jai sees them. I put father's markings on them and ...Nateeya, where is Sar jai? I have many things to show her.

(Enter Nateeya)

Nateeya. (Silent)

Mother. Are you mute child?

Nateeya. She...she's gone. She left on that ship bound for England.

Bakari. Stop your foolishness.

Nateeya. It is true.

Bakari. On a ship for England. What...why?

Mother. Oh no...no.

Nateeya. A white Doctor from England said he

wanted to put her in a show and she'd make lots of money.

Bakari. And you let her go? The white men who come here have only evil in their hearts.

Nateeya. I could not stop her.

Mother. (Lowers her head) We should not had let dem missionaries fill her head wit dey lies. First, dey make ya trust dem. Then, dey take all ya got; even ya soul. When ya sista was born, ya fata and me know she be special. Dey say, I can neva have a baby. But there she come; kickin' and screamin'. And her make a way fa you and ya brutha to come from me womb. I pray for the same God ta walk with her now.

Bakari. I will stop her. **(Spear in hand runs off stage. Then back to center stage as ship whistle blows)** Sar jai.....Sar jai **(drops head, cries and falls on his knees reaching towards the audiance)** Sar jai.

(Close Curtain))

Act II

(Scene: A corner of town in the city of London. Doctor and Shepherd wait as George brings Sarah over.)

George. You've sure got a wild heathen here, doctor. It took me a while but I was able to tame her, alright.

Doctor. I trust you've thoroughly broken her spirit?

George. Like a wild Thoroughbred ready to be saddled. Sweetest piece of...

Doctor. No need for vulgarities. I am a Christian, you know.

George. Of course, doctor. And here; before I forget **(Gives him money)**

Doctor. What's this for?

George. Your share of the booty, doctor.

Doctor. What?

George. It was a long voyage. Once the men got a whiff of this sweet thing, they dam near knocked down the door trying to get her. So I figured, why not turn a profit? And I didn't want to be greedy; so.

Doctor. I certainly hope you haven't damaged her, George. You are a bit of a brut.

George. Oh, she's just fine; aren't ya honey? **(Puts his arm around her shoulders and kisses her cheek as she pulls away.)** Here are her belongings. Where are you going?

Doctor. My where abouts are no longer your concern. After all, you've been well compensated.

George. Yes. And it's greatly appreciated. But I kind of hoped I could stop by and visit my sweet love once in a while.

Doctor. Hardly.

George. Well, anytime you need some help, don't hesitate to call on old George. Yes sir-ree.

Doctor. Indeed I will. Come along Sarah. You mustn't tarry. I need to get you fitted for costumes. The Sarah Bartman show starts very soon.

Sarah. That is not my name.

Doctor. It is your new name. All Africans deserve a good, Christian name. And you are no different, Sarah.

Sarah. I don't feel good. Those men on the ship, they...

Doctor. I am not interested in anything those fools did. I'm sure you were quite entertaining. However, we have a schedule to keep. Shepherd, put her belongings in there. This is where you shall reside until I decide otherwise. Change into these garments. Your first viewing literally starts in minutes. Shepherd, fetch me my bag.

Shepherd. Yes sir.

Doctor. Shepherd, you are charged with the task of looking after Sarah. Make sure she has food and water as needed. Change and clean her buckets. In my absence, you're to make certain no one gets too close or asks her any questions. Is that understood?

Shepherd. Yes, sir.

Doctor. I want you to position yourself here...no...no...there. And collect my money. No one gets a free peep unless I say so. Now, I need to examine Sarah. **(He enters Sarah's quarters. The curtain blocking the audience view is pulled. About one minute later he emerges.)** Shepherd put this sign up. Then go back over there and prepare yourself. **(To Sarah)** come on out and let's have a look at you. **(Sarah emerges wearing half skirt and miner covering around her breasts.)** Let these trinkets dangle from your ears. Good. Now, my Hottentot Venus, step onto your stage.

Sarah. That is a cage, sir.

Doctor. Yes.

Sarah. I'm not getting in there.

Doctor. Yes, you are. Listen Sarah, this cage merely

provides the viewer with a fear for the uncivilized environment of Africa. It's dramatic flair. It's showmanship. It's....it's...

Sarah. It is a cage. And I am not an animal, sir. I'm not getting into that cage.

Doctor. Do not think I will not use force if need be? But I want you jovial and undamaged. **(Removes contract from breast pocket)** When you signed this contract you agreed to its terms. If you break this contract, you'll receive twenty lashes and sent directly to jail. You will not get any money and you will never be able to get back home. You want to see your mother again, don't you?

Sarah. Yes, my ma-ma needs me. But you told me...

Doctor. Dam it! This is not a negotiation. Constable...I say Constable, come here.

Constable Lahey. Is everything alright?

Dotor. What is your name?

Constable Lahey. Constable Lahey at your service, sir.

Doctor. Well Constable Lahey, I have a small donation for you. **(Hands him Money)** You do an excellent job of protecting us from criminal elements throughout the city.

Constable Lahey. Thank you, sir. Me wife and lad

thank you, too.

Doctor. You're very welcome. But I have a problem that requires your assistance... and your discretion.

Constable Lahey. But of course. I'm always discreet. I've performed over a dozen abortions without a hitch. That's me; Constable by day...mad doctor with a coat hanger by night, huh. **(Slaps Doctor's back)**

Doctor. No, it is not that type of a problem. But I shall keep that in mind.

Constable Lahey. Oh.

Doctor. Allow me to explain. I am a doctor and scientist. I am a world traveler. It took us months to get back here from the dark continent; crammed aboard a ship that did not represent the modern age- mold, leaks, vermin...only to deal with the insubordination of my slave girl.

Constable Lahey. I shall have her flogged.

Doctor. No. That is not why I summoned you. Psychology is an important part of control. Where brute force is needed for the black African male of the species, we must use the African female's maternal nature against her. She is the key to our money and power. **(Whispers in Lahey's ear)**

Constable Lahey. (Walks over to Sarah) You misplaced Africans get bolder everyday; don't you!

We put Negro women in jail, too. Come with me wench.

Sarah. I don't want to go to jail. I've done nothing wrong.

Constable Lahey. He is your master. And as an officer of the law I am sworn to uphold his property rights. And while you're in jail, we will send a ship to pick up your sister and bring her here to work in your stead. Now come along.

Sarah. Please...no. **(She runs into cage and shuts door.)**

Officer Lahey. They do hold their family close. Don't they?

Doctor. Indeed. You see Sarah, the law is on my side.

Sarah. Please doctor, my sister is not part of what I've done.

Doctor. Then do as you're told and she shall be fine. Thank you Constable. That'll be all. **(Constable Lahey Exits)** You'll find that I'm easy to get along with Sarah. But do not test me. **(Locks cage and hangs key nearby.)** Shepherd, stay alert. I shall return momentarily. **(Exits)**

Shepherd. Mrs., are you hungry? Do you need something to drink?

Sarah. My name is Sar jai

Shepherd. Sar jai, I put extra straw in your cage to make it as comfortable as I could. And I have proper food. Not what we ate on the ship. It will keep you in good health.

Sarah. Thank you but no. I have no desire to eat. My belly feels like it's tied in knots. The weather here is so different; cold, damp and sad.

Shepherd. Yes, you'll have to adjust to it in time. Here in Europe, we dress in layers many months out of the year. It is nothing like the beautiful village you come from.

Sarah. You liked my village?

Shepherd. Yes, very much so. I've accompanied Dr. Dunlap on many voyages. But my eyes have yet to rest upon such beauty as your African coast. We sailed into a different world that day. A world where flowers blush in season and I felt the mist covered mountains dampen my face. Your green valleys compliment the giant trees that look as if God planted them there himself. I keep your village in a book inside my head. Your sun, always shining upon faces that smile and absorb God's rays; unforgettable. Only a fool could ignore such beauty. Your colorful garments and handmade pearl necklaces all look like paintings; stroked with the creators finest brush. To see families living, loving and working together; represents God's order. Here in Europe, I rarely see such warmth. Doctor Dunlap says the African's do not deserve such beauty. But I think him wrong because why would God put you there instead of he? **(Long pause)** Sorry, I should not have said that.

Sarah. I've never heard anyone speak like you. Are you not a poet?

Shepherd. (Bashfully lowers head) No...no.

Sarah. You should be.

Doctor. (Enters with six-year-old African boy) Shepherd, meet our little music maker. His real name was uncivilized and next to impossible to pronounce. So, we'll call him Little Buck. Little Buck is on loan to me by Sir. Wilhelm's Traveling Circus. A splendid group of chaps who know how to bring in crowds. He is a mute. That means his tongue is worthless. So, you must take good care of him. He will entertain the crowds with his Zulu drums while Sarah performs her tribal dance. It will be spectacular. Ready yourselves, it's time to start the show. **(Center stage begins yelling)**

Step right up, ladies and gentlemen. My name is Doctor William Dunlap, surgeon, academic, intellectual, scholar, world traveler, explorer and adventurer. I've ventured into the darkest regions of Africa, where few white men have dared to travel. I have fought lions and cannibals and other unimaginable horrors to bring you something never before seen in all of Europe. Ladies and gentlemen, I give you the most lustful women from the dark continent; the african princess, sex goddess, Sarah, the Hottentot Venus.

(Doctor prompts boy to beat the drums. Sarah exits cage and begins to dance for three minutes.)

(Enter 1st Woman, 2nd Woman and Researcher. They pay Shepherd and watch.)

(After the dance)

1st Woman. Oh my God. She looks angry. Is she dangerous?

2nd Woman. Look at the size of her thighs. They'll make four of mine. Look at her lips. They're so big.

1st Woman. Dear Lord. Do you see her buttocks?

2nd Woman. How can I not? That thing belongs on a donkey.

1st Woman. Or perhaps a guerilla? **(laughter)**

2nd Woman. How is she able to dance with such a deformed body?

1st Woman. Obviously when they civilized her, they taught her how to dance.

2nd Woman. Do you think the males of the species love such a thing as she?

1st Woman. Where our husbands would be sickened by such a wide backside, the African males probably adore her. After all, she must be called the "Hottentot Venus" for a reason.

2nd Woman. May we pet her?

Doctor. But of course. Sarah, be perfectly still.

2nd Woman. It's so strong and firm; like an ox.

1st Woman. (While touching Sarah's butt) I can't imagine walking with such a heavy load. You see, her shoulders are so broad. That's to accommodate the weight of her breasts.

2nd Woman. Oh yes, I see.

1st Woman. It could be centuries before they evolve into one of God's own. My church missionary work has taken me on many travels. While I have met many cultures, it is clear to me that God achieved his greatest perfection with the white race.

2nd Woman. Absolutely. **(The two women exit)**

Researcher. Those mammoth breasts could nurse at least a dozen pups. And look at that rear. It can't be real. Dunlap, this is some kind of parlor trick, isn't it?

Doctor. I assure you, sir, no trickery is involved. You may touch her if you like. Don't be shy. But be careful. Do not look directly into her eyes. They will entice the most noble of men.

Researcher. (Nods and averts his eyes) As if her dance wasn't arousing enough. **(He inspects Sarah's butt, teeth and gums)** You have quite the oddity here, sir. And I must say Doctor, you've got some guts going into the heart of Africa.

Doctor. Indeed, it was no small affair.

Researcher. Well, it paid off big. This....Sarah is a rare find indeed. Now, as a researcher I must ask? What is she like....um...sexually?

Doctor. I haven't a clue.

Researcher. Really? How can you ignore her mating dance? I'd dare say such a display would awaken the sleeping giant inside any man; who's still above ground anyways.

Doctor. You know, throughout the colony's they'd consider your proposal beastiality. In fact, in many places; illegal.

Researcher. Well I didn't mean...

Doctor. However, the British Empire is far more enlightened and I'm sure that with the right type of persuasion, arrangements can be made in the name of science. I'm more then willing to help further your

research as well as your own... primitive...
curiosities.

Researcher. (Ogles Sarah with his eyes) Yes...yes
indeed. **(Shows Doctor a large sum of money.)**
Additionally, my colleagues at the Berkshire
Research Institute will find your Sarah quite
fascinating. I'd like to have her examined by more
qualified specialists.

Doctor. I'm afraid that will not be possible. I'm in
the entertainment business and my schedule will
not permit...

Researcher. You will be paid handsomely.

Doctor. What day did you say you would like to
schedule that examination?

Researcher. Let us discuss it over a spot of tea,
shall we?

Doctor. Indeed. Shepherd?

Shepherd. Sir?

Doctor. Keep a steady eye on our Hottentot Venus.
And place her back into her cage. I shall return
shortly.

Shepherd. Yes, sir.

(Doctor and Researcher exit.)

Sarah. Shepherd, I'd like some water, please. And fresh rolls if you have any.

Shepherd. Yes, of course.

Sarah. After sixty-four days of misery on that boat, I am glad to be on dry land. My ma-ma said this was a cold country; filled with frost and hard clay. But I am not cold.

Shepherd. We have yet to see the cold season. It is bitter and long. I will make certain you are prepared.

Sarah. Back home, it is the storm season. Sometimes when it's raining and the wind blows the grain across the land, it sticks to the mud in front of our door. My little sister Nateeyah and me would run outside and dance. That warm, thick mud would gush between our toes. I know it sounds crazy but it was so much fun. My ma-ma would get her broom and chase us because... **(Starts crying)**

Shepherd. Young Miss, please don't cry.

Sarah. I can't help it. I want to go home.

Shepherd. Here, you can dry your tears with this. **(Long pause)** I knew the doctor was up to something foul. But I did not know he would put you into a cage. I am truly sorry ma'am.

Sarah. My name is Sar jai. But the doctor wrote Sarah on that sign. So, now you must call me Sarah when he is around. But I'd like to hear you say Sar jai when we are to ourselves.

Shepherd. As you wish. **(Pause)** And I'm called Shepherd. I was once named Thomas Branch and before that Kenata Bakur. My mother named me that.

Sarah. Why do you have so many names?

Shepherd. When I was one or two our new master named me Thomas. He too said it was a proper Christian name. But my mother told me to never forget my real name or where I come from. She told me to speak it everyday....to speak the names of my brothers as well. I have two brothers; both younger then I. My mother said one day we will all meet again. But in all these years, we have not. When Doctor Dunlap purchased me from my master he changed my name. He said to all Christians, Thomas represented doubt. So, he renamed me Shepherd because I reminded him of a Sheep dog.

Sarah. He bought you; like goods from a market place?

Shepherd. It was his first voyage to America and he purchased me from my master as a souvenir...a trophy.

Sarah. That's horrible. The people I knew as a girl, worked off their debts then they returned back home after a few years.

Shepherd. The type of slavery I was born into, I'm

afraid, there was no return.

Sarah. You were so young. I can only imagine how scared you must have been.

Shepherd. Not really. I was actually kind of glad. I was relieved. My former master in America was a hateful and bitter man. His life was brooding, friendless, loveless and lonely. He only kept us slaves around to abuse. His house was always dark, cold and without life. The hallways were draft filled passages that led from one cold room to the next. We were not allowed to open the shutters, and he rarely used candles at night. Every morning at sunrise I was forced to lay topless on the floor in front of his burned, oak, rocking chair; that squeaked every time it moved. He'd place his cold, damaged feet on my stomach and press firmly. At three, four and five years old I couldn't understand why. I just knew that it hurt. But master Thomas said my black belly would remove his rheumatism and gout. Sometimes, I can still feel his infected nails digging into my ribs. He had four slaves and whenever he felt so inclined he would beat us. He would beat me, kick me and throw things at me for no reason whatsoever. One morning Doctor Dunlap stopped by the plantation to get directions. My mother, knowing that master Thomas was heavily in debt, convinced him to buy me.

She feared that if I didn't get away soon, he would kill me. When I look back on it now, I realize she couldn't have been no more then eighteen or nineteen at the time; making such a heart wrenching decision. At any rate, Doctor Dunlap didn't beat me. In fact, he taught me how to read and write, shine and polish his shoes, prepare his meals, trim his hair, and how a gentleman wears a suit of clothes and top hat. A bit of astrology and arithmetic, too.

Sarah. Are you forced to he speak like him as well?

Shepherd. I don't think so.

Sarah. I was just teasing.

Shepherd. Oh **(laughter)**

Sarah. What of your mother and father?

Shepherd. I don't remember my father. But my mother is never far from my mind. She's about this tall. Her skin as soft as dry cotton; she never worked a day in the fields. Her hair and clothes always smelled of sweet cinnamon. She worked in the kitchen and cinnamon would get all over her.

Sarah. So you are owned by the Doctor?

Shepherd. Not owned. There is no longer slavery in England. However, the law reduced ownership to indentured servitude. And I have several more years to serve.

Sarah. What if you were to flee?

Shepherd. I imagine the local magistrate would issue an arrest warrant. But why would I do such a thing?

Sarah. Don't you want to be completely free?

Shepherd. Free?

Sarah. Well... yes. Free to do as you please. Free to spend your whole day fishing... hunting or swimming. If you choose to sing all day, you can do that too.

Shepherd. Sing all day, hummm. **(Laughs.)**

[Enter Doctor, Researcher, 1st Woman and 2nd Woman with examination equipment.]

Doctor. Alright, come along Sarah. **(Unlocks cage)** These good people are here to examine you. Let us step into her quarters.

Sarah. Ex...ex..amine me?

Doctor. Yes, medical research. Come inside and remove your clothing. **(Everyone but Shepherd enters into her quarters and the curtain is drawn.)**

Sarah. Owww. **(Pause)** That hurts!

Researcher. Lie back and be perfectly still.

1st Woman. So, her abnormal buttock is equally matched by her abnormally large genitals; interesting. Have you ever seen anything like this?

2nd Woman. No. They are as long as flaps on a lapel. **(Laughter.)** This needs to be documented.

Sarah. Owww, can I cover up now?

Researcher. Doctor, please control the subject. Need I remind you that we paid you a generous sum of money?

Doctor. Sarah you will lie back down and shut up at once. **(Hits her with cane.)**

Researcher. Never mind. We've seen enough here. We will continue our examination tomorrow morning on campus. **(They all exit Sarah's quarters. 1st and 2nd Woman both exit stage.)** Doctor, you have not forgotten our agreement?

Doctor. Of course not. Proceed.

(Researcher removes top hat and re-enters Sarah's quarters. There's rumbling about and Shepherd stares in horror.)

Doctor. Shepherd, I have a supply list I need filled at once. **(Hands shepherd list and sits down.)**

Shepherd. (Nods Exits)

[Researcher Emerges from Sarah's Quarters.]

Doctor. I trust your research went well?

Researcher. Quite well. However, she was still a tad bit... rambunctious. But I have something that will help alleviate that problem. **(Hands him tonic.)**

Doctor. Oh, what's this?

Researcher. Control.

Doctor. Excuse me?

Researcher. A potion of sorts; imported from the Far East. They call it opium. It will make your Sarah very cooperative. Mix it with her tea. Or for immediate results, it must be injected directly into the bloodstream.

Doctor. Yes. I've heard of this....opium. Control, yes. Thank you.

Researcher. Today there have been many things learned; many things indeed. Make certain you give her a dose before you bring her to our school tomorrow.

Doctor. Yes, of course. Until tomorrow! **(Researcher Exits)** Shepherd, I'm off to get tea and crumpets for our Sarah. I'll be back shortly. Secure her in the cage.

Shepherd. Yes, sir.

Sarah. I am not hungry.

Doctor. You must eat to maintain your strength.

Sarah. I will eat nothing you give me. I'd rather starve to death.

Doctor. So young, defiant and impetuous. Nothing at all like you huh, Shepherd? That's the stark difference between being raised in a civilized society, compared to a savage environment.

Sarah. Did you hear me? I'd rather starve.

Doctor. Oh really? If you were to die then I shall be forced to travel back to your village, retrieve your sister and put her in your stead.

Sarah. My brother will kill you.

Doctor. Really. Shepherd, this time lock that chain around her ankle. **(Exits)**

Sarah. Shepherd, I will only eat food prepared by your hands. There's too much evil in his.

Shepherd. (Nods) I understand.

[Enter Prostitute looking everything over]

Prostitute. Well, what have we here? Are you tryin'

ta move in on me territory, girl? Speak up.

Sarah. What?

Prostitute. Oh, Christ almighty! You're that freak. You're the "Hottentot Venus." Yeah, we've all heard about you. A seductress you are. They say no man can walk by you without looking at your tush. Freak or not, if ya think ya gonna take money out me garders, you're wrong, love. I'll climb in there with ya, I will.

Sarah. Really! Do you think he would let you trade places with me?

Protitute. Yeah, right. As if I'd ever get such a big bum? **(Pause)** Are you serious missy? I was just... Are ya sayin' you don't want to be in there?

Sarah. No...yes...I mean. I signed a document and now, I'm afraid the look on that man's face, and the evil in his eyes. I fear he will never let me go.

Prostitute. Just quit and go home. So let 'em sue ya.

Sarah. You make it sound so easy.

Prostitute. Silly girl, slavery was outlawed over 5 years ago in England. Didn't your mum tell ya?

Sarah. Ma-ma, oh ma-ma. **(Starts crying)**

Prostitute. Are you...you...you're crying? For God's

sake, girl, stop ya blubbering. I didn't mean
to...look. How did you get in there? Where do you
come from?

Sarah. Cape Town. Doctor Dunlap said I could
make lots of money in his show. But I have only
seen the inside of this cage.

Prostitute. A bit naive were ya? Well honey, you'll
find that all men promise ya the moon but give you
pure hell. My last husband....

Shepherd. My apologies to you ma'am, but my
master said Sarah wasn't permitted to talk to any
streetwalkers.

Prostitute. I beg your pardon. You obviously don't
know a lady when you see one. I'm no streetwalker.

Shepherd. My apologies again and no offense
ma'am but he also said no harlots, ball-breakers,
jezebels, temptresses, trollops, strumpets or ladies
of the evening; either...ma'am.

Prostitute. (Laughing) I doubt if anyone has ever
insulted me with such sincere kindness as you love.
(Rubs Shepherd's face)

Doctor. Hey you wench. What is your business
here?

Prostitute. Conversing with my new friend.

Doctor. You're a trespassing vagrant. I shall have

you thrown in jail.

Prostitute. I've been there. Done a year at Bridewell too.

Doctor. That's an appropriate facility for your kind.

Prostitute. Good Doctor, I do believe it to be illegal to simply snatch some black woman off the street and place her into a cage. **(Laughs)** There are laws. She may not know her rights, but I do. However, I can be persuaded not to advise her of said rights; if properly... motivated.

Doctor. Are you attempting to extort me? You depraved strumpet. I'll have you locked up for so long you'll forget your father's name. Although it's unlikely you ever knew it. Shepherd, get over here! **(Doctor grabs prostitute's arm)**

Shepherd. Yes, sir.

Doctor. Go fetch Constable Lahey. **(Dragging Prostitute off stage)**

Prostitute. Get ya bloody hands off me. I know people. Me best John is a lawyer. I'll tell. You can't push me around.

Doctor. Off you go. And don't come back.

Sarah. I don't want to be in here anymore. I don't want money. I just want to go home.

Doctor. You feel a bit emboldened now, do you? Never you mind the words of that worthless whore. I own you. Without my say, you will not eat. You will not drink. You will not sleep unless I ...say ...so. I'll make certain that you turn into a pile of bones inside that cage.

Sarah. You can't treat people like this.

Doctor. People. You think yourself a person? Hardly! You're a heathen... a primate. You are a spectacle that I shall display as long as I so please. God gave me power over you and your entire Negro race. Even the Pope said we must reduce you all to servitude.

Sarah. Why? Because I am African? Because my flesh is brown? Because I am a woman? Sir, you treat women like you hate us.

Doctor. I do not hate women. White women have their place in the pecking order behind white men.

Sarah. But why me? Why take me? Because I am young? Because I could not see through your lies? Because European people have never seen an African woman?

Doctor. Precisely. All are valid reasons. However, you will learn that money is the greatest motivator. When opportunity knocks, I open the door and I ask questions later. Besides, you also opened that door Sarah-with your massive breasts, oversized body, gigantic buttocks- that's only equal to your wide eyed curiosity. It's your own kindness that brought you here.

Sarah. I came into the world this way. With these eyes, this nose, these breasts. I was born African. It is through no fault of my own. Until now, I didn't know I did anything wrong. But if I were to beg your forgiveness, for being born black, will you then set me free?

Doctor. Hardly. **(Laughs)** But psychology is your strong suit; clever girl. You learn fast. I shall have to keep a more watchful eye on you.

Sarah. What if you had been covered in my black skin; and I ...your white? Would you care to be treated as you've treated me?

Doctor. Spare me the do unto others analogy.

Sarah. God sees you, sir. And he will not forget.

Doctor. Do not presume to lecture me. And what do wild heathens from the Dark Continent know of God?

Sarah. Throughout all of Africa my peoples have known God for thousands and thousands of years. It is written on the great temple walls and on the parchments of my ancestors. Do we not share the same God?

Doctor. That is indeed a probability. However, ask yourself; why did our God give me power over you?

(Pause) Unbelievable! I've been lured into a debate with an evolving primate. How amusing. But I am immune to half wit logic. **(Hits cage with cane)** You will mind your tongue with me. Or I shall hold you down and have your tongue cut from your head. **(Sarah backs up)** Good. You have another performance this evening. Earlier, I had Shepherd prepare you a traditional dish with African herbs and parsley.

Sarah. Shepherd made this?

Doctor. Yes. And for additional energy, the British Empire's most sought after tea. Drink it all. **(Places in cage and exits.)**

[Enter Shepherd and Constable Lahey.]

Constable Lahey. What seems to be the problem? Where is your master?

Shepherd. I do not know, sir.

Constable Lahey. Well, go find him.

Shepherd. Yes, sir. **(Exits)**

Sarah. (Holding her head) I do not think the food I ate agrees with me. Can you summon Shepherd?

Constable Lahey. Well, Hottentot Venus. I don't believe we've been properly introduced. Or we simply got off on the wrong foot. I don't think you've been here a good month and you're already quite famous. I hear them talk about you in restaurants, taverns and street corners. Even Father Gregory spoke your name during his sermon the other day. Well, this is my beat and everybody knows my name too.

Sarah. (Yells) Shepherd, I feel faint.

Constable Lahey. That would be from the lardin or morphine or something your master put into your tea. I observed him from over there. Those potions are thoroughly effective but highly addictive. Your Doctor Dunlap is a ruthless character.

(Sarah slumps down in cage. Constable Lahey unlocks cage and guides her into quarters.)

Sarah. (Grunts)

Constable Lahey. I can tell you are a wild one indeed. Straight from the southern tip of Africa are you?

Sarah. Yes. Yes. I need to lay down.

Constable Lahey. Not to worry love. I won't be long. All the ladies take a nap when Lahey gets done with 'em. **(Anxious)** Um, dark meat; fresh off the boat. I bet you still have that gamey taste. **(Slaps Sarah on the butt and closes curtain. After a couple of minutes he re-emerges fixing his clothes.)** You're lucky Sarah. The other officers will snatch the shillings right out of a wench's garters. But not me.

No, I don't want your money. You trollops go through a lot to earn a living. But what I do want, I get it whenever I want it. If you desire to stay out of jail and in my good graces, Sarah, it's best to assume the position whenever I come around. Alright, back into your cage; Hottentot Venus.

[Enter Shepherd and Doctor.]

Shepherd. Sarah **(After seeing Sarah face down in her cage, he stands and stares down Lahey.)**

Constable Lahey. **(Returns key to post)** And what are you staring at ...boy?

Doctor. Constable Lahey, I need a word with you. Shepherd, tend to Sarah. **(Doctor and Constable Lahey exit.)**

Shepherd. Sarah, are you alright?

Sarah. No, I don't think so. **(Laughs)**

Shepherd. Why are you laughing?

Sarah. I don't know. I can't help it. There's some strange magic upon me.

Shepherd. You must lay down and rest. **(Unlocks cage)** Give me your hand.

Sarah. You're saving me. Are you taking me home?

Shepherd. I am presently unable to do that.

Sarah. Your hands are soft, but strong. I like the way they feel upon my body.

Shepherd. Um, tha..tha...thank you.

Sarah. Thank you for helping me. My legs felt so light. **(Helps her into bed)** Shepherd, if I may say what is on my mind; you smell good. **(Giggles)** I do not mean to embarrass you. I have done nothing but breathe the foul smells of these evil men since I was taken from home; each one worse then the next. Their scent is all over me. I am afraid I may never be rid of it.

Shepherd. I shall bring you fresh, warm water and linen. I also have something called talcum powder. The English women use it after they bathe.

Sarah. Thank you for being so kind. You are the greatest person I've met since I was taken from my home. At least you do not hate me for some unknown reason.

(Shepherd exits and returns with pale of water and linen.)

Shepherd. You rest, Miss Sarah. I'll return shortly. I have errands to attend.

Sarah. Do you have a mate or children, Shepherd?

Shepherd. No. Doctor Dunlap forbids it. And I would not subject a wife to my life of servitude. Because of my indentured slave status my wife would share my debt to the Doctor. But someday, I shall take a wife and have sons and daughters. And I shall teach them much about the world around them. And with everything in me, I would never leave them. And what of you? Are you married? Do you have children?

Sarah. No. I was promised to someone. But now, he would never marry me.

Shepherd. Why not?

Sarah. Because, I am not pure. I have been touched by many. In my tribe, a woman who has done what I have is greatly hated.

Shepherd. You were an unwilling pawn. Furthermore, no one in your village can begrudge a woman with a smile so large it will make the mightiest warrior drop his shield. And eyes so beautiful and trusting they can hold your nation's most precious secrets.

Sarah. Your words are soothing yet poetic. You think I have beautiful eyes? **(She bashfully moves and looks away)**

Shepherd. Very much so. Now, it is you whom I've embarrassed. But I must leave. Doctor Dunlap will be looking for me soon. Once again, I apologize for having to lock your door from the outside.

Sarah. Good night, Shepherd.

Shepherd. Good night, Sarah. **(Exit)**

[Close Curtain.]

[Next Morning.]

Doctor. (Counting money) Shepherd, how many visitors did we have this week?

Shepherd. (Looks at ledger) One thousand- two hundred sixty nine, sir.

Doctor. Excellent! That's a forty percent increase over last week. And a fifty percent increase from the previous week. Our Sarah is my most profitable investment to date. That being the case, I want you to keep a more firm grip on her. Friday, we're off to Bristol and Liverpool. We cannot have those foul mouth bed wenches filling our Sarah's head up with foolish ideas. Can we?

Shepherd. No, Sir.

Doctor. Good. See to it. Now, get Sarah and escort her to her cage. She has a very lively schedule today. London has been bustling with excitement since she arrived.

Shepherd. Good morning, Sarah. I brought you some fresh juices. Do drink it before Doctor Dunlap sees it. He may not approve.

Sarah. Thank you Shepherd. Did you sleep well?

Shepherd. Yes. And you?

Sarah. My back aches a bit. But I'll be fine.

Shepherd. I shall fetch...I mean, I shall bring you more feathers to line your bed.

Sarah. Thank you, Shepherd.

Shepherd. I have been pondering something we talked about the other day.

Sarah. Oh?

Shepherd. You asked if I was truly free. I thought about it all night.

Sarah. I did not mean to hinder your rest.

Shepherd. You did not. For perfect dreams are created in darkness; a time for reflection and meditation.

Sarah. That, I have come to know well. But sometimes, I say things men do not think proper. I hope my words did not make you bitter towards me.

Shepherd. No...no. It is not that. You have made

me see my life through your eyes. As if to analyze my life or what is truly an illusion. The lie that has always been in front of me. My life with the Doctor is all I've ever known; after my mother. I fear that I may never be truly free from this debt that was never mine. To be free is to have your own thoughts and ideas and be able to act on them. I have come to see that my thoughts and ideas are given to me. It's true that my hands and feet are not bound, but they may as well be; if these hands and feet can only do someone else's bidding.

Doctor. Shepherd!...Shepherd! What's the delay?

Shepherd. If my grandmother was stolen and sold as property, was that not an illegal transaction? Therefore, her child or grandchild belongs not to a master but instead to the land of their origin. And you, I knew of your presence aboard that ship, yet I was powerless to help you. My stomach knotted up every time I glanced down the corridor and saw George invite men into his quarters; knowing you would be their entertainment. And now I have become your jailer; shuffling you back and forth into a damn cage.

Sarah. It wasn't your...

Shepherd. Wait...please. Last night I asked myself; why? I don't want to put you into that cage, but I fear what may happen if I do not. There is a powerful resentment rising inside of me. It grows stronger each passing day.

Doctor. Shepherd, show yourself immediately!

Shepherd. (Comes out pulling Sarah by the arm) Sorry sir. She was sleeping.

Doctor. Sarah, from this day forward, when the sun rises so shall you. Now get into your cage at once.

[Enter Husband and Wife.]

Husband. Lenora, my dear, you are so talented. Sketch a drawing of me next to the cage of the African beast.

Wife. Alright love.

Husband. Wait. **(Repositions himself and removes hat)** How do I look?

Wife. My dear, you are as handsome as ever. **(Talks as she sketches)**

Husband. Doctor, were you ever in danger during your travels throughout the Dark Continent?

Doctor. Yes, I fought death on several occasions.

Wife. When I was twelve, my uncle Thaddeus went to the dark continent never to return. He was rumored to have been eaten by cannibals.

Sarah. (Imitating the voice of a British woman) In a pot with peas and carrots for sure.

[Wife looks stunned. Shepherd laughs and draws a sharp gaze from the Doctor.]

Wife. (Surprised) Excuse me?

Husband. Pardon?

Doctor. Sorry, it's her feeding time. Quiet beast **(Hits cage with cane)**

[Sketches for a time then shows sketch to her husband.]

Husband. Outstanding! The children are not going to believe this. **(Husband and wife exit)**

Doctor. (To Sarah) You will silence yourself when people are about.

Sarah. Am I not here to make European women feel good about themselves?

Doctor. Still defiant, are we? Well, I have two very important examinations for you to attend. I shall not be worried about your disposition around the other doctors. Let me see your arm. **(He grabs her arm through the cage and injects her.)** This needle will guarantee you, Sarah, keep a docile tongue about you.

Sarah. Owww, that hurts! **(Slumps to her knees)**

Doctor. Not to worry. I'm sixty percent sure this dosage will not kill you. Now, come along. Shepherd; your assistance.

[Doctor and Shepherd remove her from cage and the three exits.]

[Enter Prostitute and Activist]

Prostitute. She's right over there.

Activist. This is an empty cage.

Prostitute. But there was a black woman being kept in here; against her will. I've seen her with me own eyes.

Activist. Well, there's a blanket and straw. But that's probably for animals. You were obviously mistaken. Perhaps you should work harder towards sobriety.

Prostitute. I haven't had so much as a thistle of wine today.

Activist. Listen, I have an important meeting with 'The Women's Right to Speak Society' and you've made me late. **(Prepares to exit)**

Prostitute. Please, wait a while. Just stand over here and you shall see. Please.

Activist. Oh, very well. But you'll not get one single shilling if you've been misleading me.

[Enter Doctor and Shepherd escorting a light headed Sarah.]

Doctor. Alright Shepherd, put Sarah back into her cage.

Shepherd. Yes, sir.

Prostitute. See, I wasn't lying to you.

Activist. (Walking over to Sarah) This is preposterous! Young woman, why are you in that cage? Who put you there? What is your name? Where are the rest of your clothes?

Sarah.   My name is Sarah. But the Doctor's medicine makes me feel outside of myself. **(Giggles)**

Doctor. You again! You were forewarned not to meddle in my affairs and you've involved your fellow harlot.

Activist. No. It is you who has courted trouble, Doctor.

Doctor. And you are?

Activist. My name is Eleanor Winchett; of the Brookshire Winchetts. I'm president of the Women's Right to Speak Society and Secretary of British Citizens United. I am also a close associate of Lord Nottingham of the British House of Commons. And I am appalled at your deplorable treatment of this woman.

Doctor. Well, Mrs. Winchett, this is none of your concern. Sarah is not British. She works of her own free will. And I have a signed, dated contract right here. **(Pulls out contract)**

Activist. Contract or not; your agreement is in violation of her civil liberties. You can not treat her in such an abhorrent manner. It's disgraceful. It's repugnant. It's downright shameful.

Doctor. (laughter) Africans have no shame. Why they're butt naked all over the place.

Activist. It is you who has no shame, sir. Young miss, are you hungry or perhaps thirsty? Has anyone harmed you?

Doctor. See here now, you are disrupting my business. I have a legal license of commerce. I can have you arrested. What is the matter with you, anyway? The people want to see her. They need to see her. And you will keep your distance.

Activist. The moment she set foot on English soil, she became protected by English law.

Doctor. What kind of lady speaks to men in such a manner as you? Where is your husband? What kind of man allows his wife to roam about the city creating havoc?

Activist. I beg your pardon?

Doctor. You should be at home minding you're young.

Activist. How dare you. You relic of a caveman. Today's women are free to come and go as they please.

Doctor. This is absolute rubbish.
Constable...Constable.

[Enter Constable Lahey]

Constable Lahey. Yes, sir.

Doctor. These people are not only harassing me, but they are disrupting my business.

Constable Lahey. Alright, you two, get a move on. **[Pats prostitute on butt]** And I'll be seeing you later.

Activist. Sarah

Sarah. Yes.

Activist. I'll be back with help. This scoundrel will not be controlling you much longer.

[Activist, Prostitute and Constable Lahey exits]

Doctor. Damn them. Shepherd, I'm going to converse with my counselor. Attend to my money......and property. And keep those meddlers away.

Shepherd. Yes sir. **(Rushes over to Sarah)** Sarah...Sarah. Are you sleeping?

Sarah. No. I feel strange; almost like I'm floating on clouds.

Shepherd. What did they do to you at that school?

Sarah. Just as before. They made me remove all of my garments; more then twenty men. They touched and laughed, poked and prodded. They touched my body like they'd never seen a woman before. They even measured my lips. Why did they care about the size of my lips, Shepherd?

Shepherd. I do not know.

Sarah. They touched me down there. Then they drew pictures of my body. And spoke as if I was an animal with no feelings inside or out. As if I was not standing there listening.

Shepherd. I am so sorry, Sarah. I cannot begin to imagine such horror and shame.

Sarah. Why are you sorry? You did nothing.

Shepherd. Exactly! I did absolutely nothing but watch. I have never done anything except what Doctor Dunlap tells me. It seems that I am unable to say no. I am like a son completely obedient to his father. Although he is not my father, he has become all I've ever known.

Sarah. It seems we are now sharing the same fate.

Shepherd. No. No. I am not locked in a cage. My hands and feet are not bound. Yet, I am a willing participant in an ongoing crime against God. I am a man, yet I have not my own voice. My mind is not my own. I live subdued inside the insanity of the Doctor's reality. Can you not see? Maybe I am insane as well; for he has truly made his insanity my reality. I stand and watch as the Doctor abuses one of God's beautiful creations. You must think lowly of me. But no less then I think of myself.

Sarah. No. I think not of you; but of God. God sees us both.

Shepherd. Then why does he not help us?

Sarah. My ma-ma says God helps us all in his own season.

Shepherd. I say, God only helps those who help themselves.

Sarah. Shepherd, why do you worry so...about me?

Shepherd. (Flustered) Your eyes have trapped me and will not let go. Some days, I long to pull apart those bars and wrap my arms around you.

Sarah. You need not hurt your hands on these bars. Come here. **(They hug and kiss passionately through the bars.)**

Shepherd. Your arms hold such warmth and caring. **(Pause)** I've never felt the embrace of a woman. Not since my childhood. You smell good. You feel good. And your skin... as soft as I imagined it would be. Your lips... are those in my dreams. I think I was smitten the day my eyes rested upon you. From what I know of Venus, you are she. You do Africa proud.

Sarah. (Pulls away) No. You cannot kiss me.

Shepherd. Why do you pull away? Have I hurt you?

Sarah. I have been soiled by many. I am unclean. That is not for a young man like you.

Shepherd. Why, because they say so? You have suffered affliction at the hands of heartless men; and overlooked by God almighty himself. No matter what was done to you- against your will, your mind and heart are pure. But now, I have become part of your tragedy. It is I who stands idle and watches, as does a child; doing nothing. I avert my eyes as these evil men and their vile intentions wound you. It is I who does not deserve to feel your touch.

Sarah. That woman said the Doctor was breaking the law. She said she was coming back to help me.

Shepherd. I am afraid Doctor Dunlap's hand is too far reaching. He is able to change things with his tongue; like no one I have ever seen. He is some how able to twist words and deeds to fit his many schemes. But this is wrong. He is wrong. I can no longer be his accomplice. I will not let you continue to suffer.

Sarah. (Yells) I miss my family so much.

[Enter Doctor]

Doctor. Family! Your family! Sarah, I just returned from Portsmouth harbor. And there were no Africans in their tiny canoes searching for you. There were no dark Negroes with long spears shouting out your name. No mother, brother or sister was there to claim you. They do not care. They have forgotten you already.

Sarah. That is not so. They do not have the means.

Shepherd. Sir, I think your ridicule causes Sarah pain.

Doctor. Oh, shut up you twit. **(Moves close to Sarah's ear)** You have been abandoned and soon forgotten. **(Laughs)** Do not let those wicked, hell bound women corrupt you Sarah. They will not fill your belly when it aches. They can not provide you with proper shelter. I do that. **(Pulls out contract)** You belong to me now. **(Yells)** To me! **(Long pause)** Shepherd, the late hour is upon us. Lock Sarah in her quarters and come along.

Shepherd. Doctor Dunlap.

Doctor. What is it?

Shepherd. I have something to say about Sarah.

Doctor. Oh, what is it?

Shepherd. She...she...

Doctor. Well, I don't have all night.

Shepherd. Sarah...needs fresh water sir.

Doctor. Well, see to it.

Shepherd. (Unlocks cage and walks Sarah into quarters.) Sarah...I...

Sarah. It's alright.

Shepherd. I am like a frightened child. I beg your forgiveness.

Sarah. No, it's alright.

Shepherd. It is not alright. Tonight, I shall pray for a stronger will.

Sarah. Then tomorrow you shall have one.

Shepherd. I do not deserve your kind words. **(Takes her hand)** I fear your optimism may be wasted on me. But I will try harder. I took the liberty of padding your pillow to make it firm.

Sarah. I will sleep well tonight.

Doctor. Shepherd, hurry-up! I swear, the more I age, the slower you become.

Shepherd. Good night, Sarah.

Sarah. Good night, Shepherd.

Doctor. (Center Stage) In the coming months, I shall make another journey to Africa. This time, I shall return with two African women from rival tribes. I shall put mud in the cage. Pit them in mock fights against each other... naked. I shall visit the Pigmy tribe and pick up a young Pigmy boy. Such an oddity will make a nice addition to my collection. I shall build bigger cages and show Europe exhibitions they could not even imagine. I will also exhibit the more primal sexual orientation of

Negroes in their natural habitats. Oh yes, I have such grand plans indeed.

(Next morning)

Doctor. Alright Shepherd, put Sarah into her cage. We seem to have visitors already.

Shepherd. Yes, Sir. **(Unlocks Sarah's door and enters)** Sarah, are you awake?

Sarah. Good morning Shepherd. Yes, I'm ready.

Shepherd. You seem to be in better spirits.

Sarah. Yes, I slept well. And because of you, I feel a spirit of hope.

Shepherd. Well, off you go then.

Sarah. Wait, I have something I must give you.

Shepherd. What?

Sarah. This. **(Kisses him)**

Shepherd. A morning kiss! I have seen many in my life. I never imagined getting one. What a pleasant surprise.

Sarah. Sorry. I should not have done that. I do not want to take your mind off your work. But I was unable to stop myself. All night I've thought of you;

your words yesterday. They kept my heart warm through the night. When I think about home and my family, I feel covered with sadness. I feel lost. **(Pause)** But then I think of you. Your smile, your voice, your shine, and I feel so much better. Thank you for treating me like a human being.

Doctor. Shepherd, hurry up.

Shepherd. No, it is I who must thank you.

Sarah. Why?

Shepherd. For opening up my eyes. I can now see everything. It is as if I have been sleepwalking in a fog. But it is clear to me now. What I must do. What freedom is and how it must be achieved. It must be taken; by force if need be. Because freedom is not you in a cage. It is not me putting you in that cage. It is not Doctor Dunlap commanding us. But it is we commanding ourselves. Our days and our nights should be ours to do with as we please. Tomorrow will be different for both of us.

Sarah. What do you mean?

Shepherd. I shall explain later. Come along. **(Puts her in cage)**

[Enter Prostitute, Activist and Judge]

Prostitute. Look, that's her.

Activist. And that's him. And there's that deplorable cage. You see, they just put that African woman inside of it.

Judge. Dunlap, is it?

Doctor. Yes.

Judge. I am Lord Thurston Henry; British citizen and judge. And I've come to bare witness to this despicable, senseless exhibition for myself.

Doctor. Despicable! Senseless you say? The only spectacle is the spectacle of fact and truth, sir. These women, who are determined to interfere in my affairs, have misled you for their own nefarious reasons.

Judge. How So? Unless my eyes are not my own, you sir, have an African woman locked in that cage.

Doctor. This is a show...a feature...an oddity. You've never seen a buttock's like that before. She is here for your benefit. The benefit of science. The benefit of all superior minds. This is in tribute to the white woman's perfect body. White men and women are able to love themselves more deeply; seeing the opposite of their own splendor. All things were not made in God's image. Hence, this African woman is on display.

Activist. I think this exhibition is for the benefit of your pocketbook and your sinister ego.

Doctor. I have a binding and legal contract with Sarah.

Activist. I've since learned about your dubious contracts.

Doctor. We need not this woman to stand among men and speak in such a manner. You, Mrs., would be more beneficial to your husband preparing his meals and seeing to his needs; instead of pursuing these unhealthy outside interests.

Activist. You cave dwelling cretin. I'll have you know...

Judge. Enough! We shall keep this matter civil. Doctor, regardless of your intentions or your so called contract, it is unlikely she was even eligible or intelligent enough to sign such a document. No matter, my interest lies in the laws of England and in the implementation of such laws. In three days time, a special counsel will debate if you've broken any laws or violated this woman's civil rights.

Doctor. Rights! What rights? **(Laughs)** Even now many of her people are slaves in America. And in Arabia. And until a few years ago, right here in merry old England. In fact, if I recall sir, many Negroes were slaves within your very own household.

Judge. They were willed to me by inheritance.

Doctor. How does one inherit people legally, sir? Is it the same way one inherits their father's land and title? Your laws allowed you to inherit African flesh? But we commoners had to purchase our own.

Judge. Mind your tongue, Doctor! **(Pause)** It's true. We all bare the gruesome marks of slavery; **(Points)** her dark skin most of all. And for that we shall all be judged. However, wiser hearts and minds have prevailed. We cannot redo yesterday but we can change all of our tomorrows. That peculiar institution of slavery is no more in England. And I bid it a good farewell. And you Doctor, will not turn back the hands of time. We are a country of laws and government. And by them we shall all abide; especially you sir. Good day. **(Judge and Activist exits)**

Prostitute. I bet you wish you'd given me that money now, don't ya love? **(Pokes out tongue and Doctor raises cane and chases her off stage.)**

Doctor. I'll have you flogged, wench! **(Center stage)** This is most unsettling. I am being harassed by envious zealots and do-gooders. They speak of government and laws. Simple code words to restrict my livelihood. I give the people what they want. Those who are afraid to set foot on a fishing pier more or less on a ship bound for other lands, are able to bare witness to this Hottentot woman's body. I am a good Christian and just because I choose to display this heathen as a wild animal I am suddenly classified as a villain? Rubbish. **(Pause)** However,

this does create a dilemma. **(To audience)** Do you think those hypocrites would have me charged with a crime? I've invested time and money into this venture; and made quite a tidy sum too. But...
(Pause and raises finger) That's it! I have the perfect solution. I shall sell her for a king's ransom and eliminate this problem all together. And there's not a damn thing anyone can do about it either.

Shepherd. Sarah.

Sarah. Yes.

Shepherd. Doctor Dunlap is up to something. When he gets that look and twitch about him, something is stirring.

Sarah. What is it?

Shepherd. I do not know. But it is never good. Not to worry. We will not be here to find out.

Sarah. What do you mean?

Shepherd. Until I met you, I thought my daily servitude, being the same as all the Negroes around me, was the natural order of things. My loveless life, afraid to show passion or tenderness, is all I've ever known. Since I was a child, I have obeyed nothing other then the Doctor's orders. I was an empty vessel filled daily, then consumed. But the wind of change has arrived. And Sarah you are that wind. I now intend to be the narrator of my own book. Yes, perhaps even the sole contributor to my own life's story.

Sarah. Are you alright?

Shepherd. We are a lot alike; you and I. **(Touches her face)** I'm taking you away from here.

Sarah. You're taking me back home; back to my village?

Shepherd. Some day, but tomorrow we must get away from this place and never look back. Something in me has awakened. I will not let you go. I feel tingling in my stomach and chest when I think of you. I care deeply for you, Sarah.

Sarah. As I for you. But where will we go? How will we live?

Shepherd. We can go anywhere. Anywhere our feet take us. We are free. Not pawns. I will work as I must. I am familiar with all forms of domestic labor. Even things Doctor Dunlap would not approve of. If we stay together and work together, we will be alright.

Sarah. I know how to make garments and necklaces out of beads and shells. I can prepare all of our food and make drinks out of berries and vines. I will teach you how to live off the land as we do.

Shepherd. This is no Garden of Eden like where you come from. But I will welcome your knowledge and teachings.

Sarah. We will do whatever we must. Oh Shepherd, I am so happy. Can we not leave now?

Shepherd. No. The Doctor is too watchful. I also must gather my belongings. I have money hidden away from Dunlap's greedy hands. But tomorrow at this time, we will be far away from this place; away from his devilish tricks and evil deeds. And no one shall touch you or hurt you again. Do you hear me? I will not let them. **(Takes her hand)** We will not wait for the afterlife to be content. We shall find happiness in this life as well.

Sarah. Oh yes! **(Kisses him through the bars)**

Doctor. Come along, Shepherd. I have some planning to do. There will be no exhibit today. Lock Sarah back up and let's go.

Shepherd. Yes sir. Come on, Sarah. **(Walks her into her quarters)** Tomorrow shall be a great day for us.

Sarah. I will be ready Shepherd. I will dream of you all night. As if you were lying next to me.

Shepherd. And likewise, I shall do the same. **(They kiss)**

Sarah. Good night, Shepherd.

Shepherd. Good night, Sarah. **(Exits)**

[Next morning enter Doctor; unlocks door]

Doctor. Sarah

Sarah. Yes. I'm ready to go and...

Doctor. Go where?

Sarah. (Backs up in Shock) To work sir.

Doctor. Well...good. Today, you be on your very best behavior. I have an important guest anxious to see you. I'll have none of your complaining or back talk. Or I will be forced to thrash you with my cane.

Sarah. (Nods head)

Doctor. Well, come along. Get in there. **(Pushes her down)**

Shepherd. (Enters) Sir, must you be so rough with Sarah?

Doctor. I'll handle my property any way I so choose. And furthermore... why Shepherd, I think you've taken a fancy to our young Sarah. **(Pause)** Silly me! Of course you have. It's been some time since I plucked you from your mother's breast. You are about seventeen...no eighteen? I forget. You've never tasted the sweet fruits of a woman. But you are at the age of wonder and experiment. Ready to test out your equipment, huh? Any good master would have already allowed you to sew your African oats. Well, mind your place and maybe later I'll let you have a taste of our sweet Sarah. God knows everyone else has. **(Laughs)** My virgin servant.

Sarah. Doctor, I am hungry. May I have food now?

Doctor. Did I not just warn you to behave? Shepherd, fetch Sarah some fruit. I shall return momentarily. **(Exits)**

Shepherd. Sarah, are you alright?

Sarah. I'm sorry. This morning I thought the Doctor was you coming to rouse me. I did not mean to...

Shepherd. Not to worry. It is but a small thing. However, we must hasten our steps. We leave now! **(Unlocks cage and places blanket around Sarah's shoulders.)** This will keep you warm.

Sarah. Thank you. But it is your heart that gives me warmth. Warmth I feel from the inside out. My ma-ma would have liked you Shepherd. **(Kisses him)**

Shepherd. Come along. We must hurry. **(He takes Sarah's hand and proceeds across stage.)**

[Enter Doctor and Culvier]

Culvier. I've been searching for weeks to find a new attraction.

Doctor. Excellent, as you well know, all of London has been bustling with excitement over seeing my Sarah. You'll be making money hand over fist. **(Sees Shepherd)** Shepherd, what in the bloody hell are you up to?

Shepherd. (Pauses) Sarah and I are leaving... together.

Doctor. Have you gone mad?

Shepherd. Sarah and I are leaving.

Doctor. Leaving? Rubbish. I own both of you.

Shepherd. (Unsure) No...no! You do not own me. And you do not own her. You will no longer display and shame her as you have done.. Sarah and I are leaving.

Doctor. Stop saying that! According to the laws of this land I own you for another twenty-five years. Shepherd, what has possessed you? Are you not happy? Do I not take care of you?

Shepherd. Happy! Happy to be your man servant until one of us dies? I should find happiness in that?

Culvier. Perhaps I should comeback later.

Doctor. Sir, I assure you. This shall all be resolved momentarily.

Shepherd. Please move out of our way, Doctor.

Doctor. (Sympathetic voice) Shepherd, my first words were a bit hasty. **(Pulls out contract)** I have a contract with Sarah. Do you want her to go to prison?

Shepherd. She's not going to prison. She's going with me. **(Uses stick to keep him at bay.)**

Doctor. Why, you ungrateful, disloyal dog. After all that I've done for you. This is how you repay my kindness? I could have tied you up and fed you bread and water from troth. However, I did neither. I could have beaten and brutalized you. However, I rarely struck you. Did I?

Shepherd. You struck me not with your hands but with your tongue.

Doctor. I raised you. I bartered for your purchase. When you were a child being molested and beaten by your master, I rescued you

Shepherd. I thanked you for that. I repaid you with years of loyal and mindless service.

Doctor. Mindless is right. You were an animal. A bastard. A dunce. I fed you. I clothed you. I educated you.

Shepherd. You gave me education and then withheld opportunity. And for that I should be grateful? Happy to be your servant forever?

Sarah. Shepherd, let us go now!

Doctor. (Points to Sarah) It was she. That Hottentot woman has corrupted you, Shepherd. She has misled you with her insatiable wilds. **(To Sarah)** Get back into your cage at once. **(Grabs her arm)**

Shepherd. Get your hands off her! **(He and Doctor tussle over Sarah)**

[Enter Constable Lahey.]

Constable Lahey. What's going on here?

Doctor. They have stolen my money and are trying to flee. Quickly, grab them.

Shepherd. Run Sarah!

Constable Lahey. [Grabs Sarah and Shepherd] Hold still, boy! **[Sarah bites Constable Lahey and he slaps her. A furious Shepherd begins choking him. He falls to his knees.]**

Culvier. You've lost control of your Negroes, Doctor.

Doctor. My God, Shepherd! Have you gone mad?

Sarah. Shepherd, no! **[Doctor subdues Sarah from behind and Shepherd stops choking Lahey to help her.]** Run shepherd, run!

Shepherd. No, I will not leave you.

Constable Lahey. **[Coughing]** We're going to hang you. You black bastard.

Sarah. Please, you must or they will kill you. Go!

Shepherd. [Releases Sarah's hand] I will return for you, Sarah. I will be find you. I promise. **[Exits]**

Doctor. (To Constable Lahey) Place her back into that cage.

Culvier. And what of your Negro?

Doctor. He shall be punished severely. He will not get far with a bounty on his head.

Culvier. An interesting turn of events. You almost lost your cash cow, Doctor.

Doctor. Everything is under control now. Go ahead. Inspect the goods if you like. I expect fair exchange, mind you.

Culver. Hummmm. **(Inspects her body)** Now, I'm very curious to find out what she has that everyone desires. And look at that magnificent derriere. It has freak show written all over it.

Sarah. You cannot keep me here. It is against your laws. Shepherd will return for me.

Doctor. Rubbish. Hell face charges for attempting to murder an officer of the law. You infected poor Shepherd with your animal magnetism.

Sarah. No, I cured him of your sickness.

Doctor. Cure yourself then heathen. I'll get another Shepherd. I'm sure there's another Negro for sale somewhere nearby.

Culvier. Spirited isn't she?

Doctor. Indeed.

Constable Lahey. I can close her mouth. **[Raises nightstick]**

Culvier. No. Do not harm her. **(Ogles her body. And tries to squeeze her buttocks but Sarah moves.)** Hottentot Venus indeed. An African named Sarah is as believable as a Hebrew named Matthew. That is not her real name is it Doctor?

Doctor. I stripped her of her birth name. You see Culvier, you must sever the identity, family attachments, and the future aspirations of your captive if one truly intends to control them. Thereby, they lose any sense of who they are and eventually why they are.

Culvier. You are a shrewd one, Doctor, for she is a

rare find indeed. Tell me sir, why then are you so anxious to depart with her? You've been doing quite well financially.

Doctor. Well, um, let's just say I have more lucrative business interests to pursue.

Culvier. And what of your financial arrangements with her? Surely she desires to be compensated?

Doctor. She can desire whatsoever she wants. And who's going to question my contract with an African? Just tell anyone who preys that she sent all of her money home to her family. **(Pause)** Look Culvier, if you do not wish to purchase....

Culvier. Consider her sold.

Doctor. What?

Culvier. (Extends hand) Sold! Now, let us negotiate the terms over a spot of tea; shall we? I am sure you can use some.

Doctor. Yes. Yes indeed. Constable, would you be so kind as to keep a watchful eye on things here?

Constable Lahey. I don't see why not. **(Opens hand for payment)**

Doctor. (Pause) Very well! **(Gives him money)** And administer this if she continues to be belligerent. **(Hands him the opium)**

[Doctor and Culvier exits]

Constable Lahey. (Silently Smirking) Alone at last! I feared they would never leave. My sweet tooth is acting up. Do you have something sweet for Constable Lahey?

Sarah. No, stay away from me.

Constable Lahey. Oh don't be that way. **(Keeps reaching through the bars)**

Sarah. I said do not touch me!

Constable Lahey. So, you would prefer to do it the hard way, do you? Give me your arm. **(Lahey snatches her arm through the bars and injects her wih the opium.)** As tame as a kitten now, aren't you love? **(Unlocks cage)** Come along. **(He guides her into quarters as the curtain blocking audience view is drawn. Sarah begins laughing.)** What are you laughing at wench?

Sarah. I remember you now. Your name is tiny. **(Opium makes her scratch her giggle)**

Constable Lahey. Why you insolent, black whore. Do you know who I am? I am the law. You can't speak to me in such a manner. I'll teach you your place. **(Drags Sarah out of quarters and is slapping her around.)**

[Enter Doctor]

Doctor. What ills you man? Put Sarah back into her cage.

Constable Lahey. Damn heathen bit me again.

Doctor. Perhaps you should remain at arms distance and not remove her from her cage. What if she had run off?

Constable Lahey. She would not get far. I administered a dose of this potion.

Doctor. Listen Lahey, there are countless strumpets around here. Yet you are not content with them. You cut into my profits every time you remove her from that cage.

Constable Lahey. I was just...

Doctor. I know what you were just... doing. It is not what I pay you for. Now, if you will excuse me.

Constable Lahey. (Hits cage with blackjack) I'll be seeing you later...Hottentot Venus. **(Exits)**

Doctor. Not to worry, Sarah. He will not be seeing you later. I just sold you to a Frenchmen named Culvier. That's the gentleman you met earlier. All my troubles are over. I no longer have to worry about people meddling in my affairs or being pressed by the authorities. You girl, will be taking a long trip tomorrow.

Sarah. No...no...no. It cannot be.

Doctor. Yes...yes.... yes. I was paid quite handsomely too. **(Pause)** What, nothing witty to say? Oh, cheer up. You're going to like France. I personally find the French morally depraved. But who am I to judge?

Sarah. I am afraid my love may never find me in France.

Doctor. Will you stop it! Your love indeed! Utter nonsense! What does an animal know of love? Your instincts are primal; more lustful.

Sarah. Yet you are talking and explaining to an animal. You are loud and wrong. Who is the greater animal; me inside this cage or you who put me here? The feeling I have in my heart; it hurts now that Shepherd has gone away. My spirit flew high when he touched my hand or kissed my lips. That is love, sir; something that a cold heart such as yours will never know. And if Shepherd has that same feeling inside of him, our spirits will find each other no matter what you do.

Doctor. Foolish girl! It is but lust you feel for Shepherd and he for you. I believe the question was what idiot would believe a heathen such as you knows of love?

Sarah. You keep using words such as animal and heathen. But from the moment we met, you were the animal seeking to devour me. I gave you water and you kidnapped me. I gave you trust and you put me in this cage. You and those like you are heathens. Your heart knows not mercy or shame. You plan war and suffering and pillaging and rape. I think it is because you want be noticed by God.

Doctor. Well, Sarah, I own and feed you. So to you, I am God.

Sarah. Your destruction of the innocent and your abuse of the young hands you a strange pleasure. That is not of God. You offer only pain to those you think less of; instead of just letting them be. That is not of God. You sir, have no soul and it hurts. Your hollow heart is unhappy and empty. Your insides are as a dry well filled with earth.

Doctor. Oh, shut up!

Sarah. But making others suffer will only bring you temporary relief. By sunset tomorrow, your empty soul will once again ache through the night.

Doctor. (Yelling) You Africans are not part of humanity. That is why enslavement is good for the African.

Sarah. Some of the people who walk by here do not see a naked woman, a freak, an animal, or a beast in a cage. They see me, Sar jai; a strong, beautiful, African woman. And they see you; a hurting, lonely, evil man who has made money his God. **(Pause and emphasize)** I pity you.

Doctor. You pity me. Shut up beast!

Sarah. Say it louder, Doctor. Horrible things are easy to believe if you say them loud enough.

Doctor: You dare taunt me? Shut up! **(He's unhinged)**

Sarah. **(Sarah laughs)** My ma-ma was right about you.

Doctor. **(Composes himself)** They usually are.

[Spotlight on Sarah as singer enters and sings 'Motherless Child.' Sarah cries, yells, grabs bars; showing her pain, anger, misery, frustration and helplessness within the cage.]

[Song ends. Close curtain.]

Act lll

(Scene: A street with a park bench. Sarah walks painfully down the street and into her flat; holding the arm of a man. When they emerge, he pays her, tips his hat, and they go in opposite directions off stage. Prostitute enters holding the arm of a man. They go into Sarah's flat. When they emerge, he pays her, tips his hat and they go in opposite directions off the stage. Sarah and prostitute enter stage casually walking together and talking.)

Prostitute.   You could say I inherited the family business from me mum, after some local bloke sliced her face. No John wanted to be seen with her after that. And since we still had to eat, here I am; twenty-five years later. Sarah, I've always wondered, what did you do when they took you to France? You rarely speak of such things, but if you care not to, I understand.

Sarah.   No, it's alright. You are my best friend, Nancy. I tell you everything. **(Pause)** After I arrived in France, I was sold four more times. I was in a traveling circus for a bit, too. It was better than being alone in those dark, smoke filled rooms. I was one of the side show freaks. I just stood in my cage as rich people pointed and stared and touched. Sometimes the ring master made me wear costumes and masks. Or they put chains on me and told the people I was a dangerous animal.

Sometimes I charged from my cage like a bull. People would usually run. Seeing white people running scared always made me laugh. And some of the people who threw bananas at me, well I threw them right back at them. The ringmaster liked it. He said it made the crowd...riled up, is what he called it. But in the end, they had the best laugh because they went home after the show. I did not.

Prostitute. Christ almighty, I would've killed my self.

Sarah. (Shrugs) I didn't care. I had lost all hope. You and I both know what a woman can get through, and get used to over time. I even got use that cold, damp cage filled with straw. I stayed naked so much that when I did put clothes on it felt strange. I didn't feel so out of place amongst others like me.

Prostitute. Others?

Sarah. Those who are different; oddities is what the ring master called us. There was one man with hair covering his entire body like a wolf.

Prostitute.   Oh my god, even his face?

Sarah.   Yes, even growing out of his ears. And yet, another man that was so tiny he only came to my knees. There was a fat woman named Wilma who had a sign that said she weighed a thousand pounds.

Prostitute. My God!

Sarah.   It's alright. She told me she only weighed six hundred. **(They laugh)** There were all sorts of people from all over the world. During the day, when others were not watching, we played cards, told jokes, and jumped up and down on the trampolines. We drank hordes of liquor each night before the show opened. They were a good lot. We were all different; yet the same. I sure miss them. **(They sit down on the bench and Sarah looks sad.)**

Prostitute.   Oh, cheer up, love. You've still got me, and I can play cards and I'll let you win. **(They laugh)** Oh, and that reminds me. **(Hands her a bottle of liquor)** Happy birthday love!

Sarah. How did you......

Prostitute. See, old Nancy never forgets.

Sarah. Thank you. **(they hug)** You are a good friend, Nancy.

Prostitute. Well, pop it open. I bought that yesterday from a very expensive shop on Seventh Avenue.

Sarah. (Sarcastically) Bought it? Did you?

Prostitute. Alright, stole it! The shop keeper chased me three blocks for my trouble. So, you'd better enjoy it. **(They both laugh and drink passing the bottle back and forth.)**

Sarah. I think we did pretty well tonight. **(Counts the money)**

Prostitute. It's the best I've done in weeks! You're me good luck charm, you are.

Sarah. I still have so much more to save.

Prostitute. Not to worry love. You'll get it! Just stay close to old Nancy and you'll be on that ship headed back to Africa in no time.

(Enter Stranger)

Stranger. Are you the nymph they call Sarah Bartman?

(Sarah nods).

Stranger. Well, good. Come along, and give me your autograph when we finish. It's for my scrapbook.

(Pause) Well, I haven't got all night.

Sarah. Come back tomorrow, sir. I'm done for the evening.

Stranger. Hog wash. I'm not waiting until tomorrow. **(He pats his foot)** I'll pay extra.

(Sarah doesn't respond but continues drinking.)

Prostitute. Listen sir, she said no!

Stranger. Well, what about you?

Prostitute.   I'm closed.

Stranger. Rubbish. Wenches never close their legs.

Prostitute. (Jumps up with bottle in hand) Go away or I'll bash your skull and you'll have to explain to your misses why you were on Bute Street this hour of the night.

[Stranger runs off.]

Sarah. They are all the same aren't they?

Prostitute. I've been working the streets since I was thirteen and the men never change. They only get cheaper.

Sarah. Nancy, have you ever thought about how quickly things turn bad? We should hold close the time we spend with those we love; you know? Find comfort in their arms. When I was young, I...

Prostitute. When you were young? You're only twenty-one, love; with plenty more lively days ahead of you then old Nancy. What's bothering you, honey?

Sarah. I feel old. I feel like my youth has passed me by. I think my fast life has caught up to me. My soul is worn and my heart beaten down by disappointment. My youth was stolen the day I was spirited on board that ship.

Prostitute. I've never been on a ship. Never been anywhere; except here. Bet it was hell. Stuck on a ship and surrounded by water, with a bunch of drunken sailors pawing at you. I can't imagine spending day after day, week after week with the likes of those blokes.

Sarah. Until then, I'd never been on anything bigger then my brother's raft. For the first week I was scared, dizzy and my food kept coming back up. But that made no difference to those...those foul smelling men who entered my cabin. Night after night, no matter how often I vomited, it didn't stop them from taking me. I even threw up on them and all they would do is laugh and squeeze me harder.

Prostitute. My God!

Sarah. God. No. I think that was when I first realized God had abandoned me.

Prostitute. Don't say such things. Neither God nor I will ever abandon you, Sarah; ever. He saved you from that cage and that wicked, crazy Doctor. He's got me looking after you, he does. Now you're here, working for yourself. You're a business women, like me, you are.

Sarah. For a long time I felt shame. It was a heavy shame that no woman...no human being should be made to suffer. My spirit was tied...broken, and my hope of freedom beaten and drained from me. Some days I found myself outside that cage, standing among the crowd; staring in and laughing at my own butt, breasts and lips. I became the ugly beast they needed me to be. I had truly given up.

Prostitute. God! All those people looking and touching. It had to be an absolute nightmare; night after night.

Sarah. A nightmare during the day as well. It was unbearable, once Shepherd was gone. You know, I was sold to a wealthy landowner once, who kept me around to amuse and entertain his friends. During a thunder storm one night I begged God to kill me. Strike me down. Send me to a better life. But he would not do it. The following night a well dressed businessman entered my cage; looking for some fun. I also begged him to kill me when he was finished doing his business. I didn't know it at the time but he had come there with his wife who was off to the side; hiding and watching.

Would you believe it was she who commanded her husband to purchase me. It was she who handed me the key to my cage. **(Shows key on chain around her neck)** Early the next morning she wrapped me in a scarf and veil. Then she whispered softly in my ear: "Leave France and never return." I guess it was the guilt she felt from staring into my eyes. But I'd like to think it was God's voice telling her what to do. And maybe he cared about me again.

Prostitute. You're a survivor, Sarah. The greatest survivor I've ever known. If I could read or write, I'd write a book about you, I would. **(Drinks and passes the bottle)**

Sarah. No one would believe you.

Prostitute.   I cannot stomach seeing anything in a cage now. And I will never set foot in a zoo again.

Sarah. It was in a cage that I learned how to gather strength from pain. I learned how to separate my mind from my body. Soon, it was not me that they touched and groped every day, but an empty body; free of it's soul. My mind learned how to escape that cage. And the very first place I went was home; to Africa. I watched my family plant corn and rice and sing the songs our fathers sang. I saw my brother fishing with his new wife and baby boy.

I stared into the face of my sister standing next to a very tall, handsome man. He must have been her husband. **(Pauses Drinks)** Sometimes, I was a wingless creature who flew above the tallest buildings in London and Paris. Dancing in fountains and perched upon trees. Other days I was a beautiful, black horse, running in fields overflowing with yellow flowers and green grass. Some nights, my cage became a castle, and I; a princess. The people passing by were my subjects. It was not bananas and peanuts that they threw but rose peddles and sunflowers. **(Pauses drinks and laughs)** I know I sound mad, but it was not hope which kept me alive, it was the wonderful journeys my mind took me on.

Prostitute. I used to do that with me johns; pretending I was not there and it was not me they were on top off. Until one day I was off pretending and some bloke's wife busted in on us waving a butcher's knife. She stabbed me in me bum on the way out of a second story window. After that, I kept me eyes on the door. **(Deep laughter)** Oh, cheer up love. Let us have no more talk of such painful times. It is your birthday. Drink up!

[Sarah holds her abdomen while wincing in pain.]

Prostitute. I wish you would go see a doctor about that pain.

Sarah. You know how I feel about doctors Nancy. I don't want their filthy hands touching me.

Prostitute. Please Sarah. They're not all bad. I'm so

worried about you. I promise to go with you. **(Pause)** Please.

Sarah. Alright.

Prostitute. Tomorrow then?

Sarah. Yes, yes. I will go tomorrow.

Prostitute. Good. **(Hugs her)** Best be on me way. Old Nancy has further business to take care of. It's getting a wee bit chilly. I'm going to get my fur coat.

Sarah. The one you got chased eight blocks for?

Prostitute. That would be the one. **(They laugh)**

Sarah. Yeah, now that you've gotten me drunk, you're going to leave. Thank you for my birthday gift. I don't recall getting a birthday gift in years.

Prostitute. Well, happy birthday love. **(They hug and prostitute exits)**

Sarah. Goodnight Nancy.

[After turning the bottle up to her head, Sarah winces in pain. She closes the door and falls across the bed. She moans in agony. Spotlight opens on her mother a few feet outside her door. Mother is humming a song and is dressed oddly; half English and half African clothing-preparing a meal.]

Sarah. Who is there? Is someone out there? **(Sarah limps painfully to the door and cautiously peeks out.)** Ma-ma is that you? Is it really you? It is! **(Hugs her)** Ma-ma I thought I'd never see you again, ma-ma. I've missed you so much. Are you here to take me home?

Mother. Child, I am home. It be you who is far away.

Sarah. But how are you in front of me? Why are you dressed so.... oddly? What of Nateeya and Bakari?

Mother. Ahhhh **(shakes head)** Dem miss ya so much when ya gone. Ya brother blame himself fa not being there. But him married now; got two little ones of his own to look after. Him name de oldest Sar jai after his big sista. And ya little sista...oh Natee make herself so much money sellin' and tradin' dem goods in the marketplaces. First, she start wit necklaces and trinkets and stones and herbs. Den her move up ta goats and chickens and corn and garments. Her so big now ya know, she got two, three helpers. Her say she make you proud when you git back home. **(Lifts Sarah's chin)** Ya be drinkin' spirit water, huh?

Sarah. My stomach pains me so bad, ma-ma. Some days I can barely walk. They have no herbs or vines here for me to heal myself. **(Wincing in pain)** The spirit water helps me when it hurts. It also helps me forget what they did. What they all did.

Mother. Ya not be minding ya fruits, huh girl?

Sarah. Ma-ma, they took me and I could not stop them. They were like wild animals; taking me and taking me. After a while, I did not care. I hated them but I hated myself even more for believing the lies. You told me ma-ma. You warned me. Some nights I sleep in darkness because I cannot bear to see myself. **(Pause)** I have reaped shame upon my ancestors and upon my father and upon you, ma-ma. For your shame I grieve. **(Pause)** Do you still love me ma-ma?

Mother. Oh, yes child. Yes. Me neva stop lovin' ya.**(Hugs her)** You are mine Sar jai; me first born. Of me flesh and blood you are.

Sarah. I'm tired ma-ma; so very tired. My pain is deep and unbearable. And my body is always aching. I want to go home ma-ma. **(Crying)** Please take me home.

Mother. Well, come along then, child. **(Leading Sarah by the hand)**

(Sarah....Sarah. Shepherd's voice off stage.)

Sarah. (Looking all around) Shepherd?

[**Sarah turns back around and her mother is gone. Holding her stomach, she stumbles back**

into her quarters and falls to the floor. Enter shepherd carrying flowers. He sits on the park bench in frustration.]

Shepherd. Time after time when I was able, I have searched for you, Sarah. But now, I fear I will never rest my eyes upon you. Oh how I curse the day I let go of your hand; tears on your face and fear upon mine. The stain of cowardice has since been upon my head; branded into my conscience like God cursing Cain. Perhaps I was not worthy of such love? The freedom I have since known rightfully belongs to you. **(Pause)** The shadow of regret troubles me...haunts me...stalks me. **[Enter prostitute]** Excuse me, madam, I was told Sarah Bartman once lived around here. Do you know where she may have gone?

Prostitute. Gone! What do you mean, sir? Me good friend Sarah lives but over there. You look very familiar to me. Nancy never forgets a face. Anyway, I'm going to check on her. You may tag along if you choose honey.

[Shepherd runs ahead of her and bangs on the door.]

Shepherd. Sarah...Sarah.

Prostitute. (Pushes him aside and enters quarters.) Oh my God, Sarah!

Shepherd. Is there a doctor nearby?

Prostitute. I'll find one. You hang on, love.

Shepherd. Sarah, it is me, Shepherd. **(Helps her into bed)**

Sarah. Shepherd, my love. I knew you would find me. You look so strong, so fit and well. **(Coughing)**

Shepherd. What ails you, Sarah?

Sarah. I know not. But my insides burn like there is a fire in the pit of my belly. I cannot make my legs move and my arms are as heavy as logs. **(Pause)** Oh listen, my ma-ma is outside waiting for me. She's come to take me home, Shepherd.

Shepherd. No Sarah, no. Stay here with me.

(Mother is humming off stage.)

Sarah. Can you not hear her singing? It is the sound of Africa. It is the sound of my home.

Shepherd. (Crying) Oh Sarah. My sweet Sarah. No.

Sarah. Why do you cry my love?

Shepherd. I have kept you in my heart all these years. I have saved a thousand kisses for this day; dreaming that I would again hold you in my arms. And now...

Sarah. Now, we are in each other's arms. Are we not? It was thoughts of you that kept me sane all these years. But now I shall shed this dark skin and bruised body and be free of this life. Free from stares and schemes and laughter and hate. **(Moans in pain)** We shall love again on the other side; for we shall know each other well in the next life, Shepherd. In the next life we shall both be free. **(She dies in his arms)**

Shepherd. **(Cries out in an agonizing voice)** Sarah. **(Murmurs)** Sarah. **(Rubs her hair and caresses her face)**

[About 45 seconds pass. Enter Doctor and Culvier.]

Doctor. No, I rarely talk about it but I started my career as a Doctor aboard a slave ship. I was tasked with seeing to the crew and sometimes its cargo. I decided life or death on many occasions. If I concluded that a Negro was too sick to complete the voyage, he was tossed overboard. And the sharks would have their fill. But I made more off Sarah Bartman then all my voyages.

Culvier. What does Bartman mean anyway?

Doctor. A euphemism for nothing. **(Laughs)**

Culvier. Take heed Dunlap, I have no interest in entering into a business arrangement with you. I find your ethics; deplorable.

Shepherd. My good man, were you not told, Ethics and morals are the true enemies of capitalism? But isn't that the pot calling the kettle black? I've since been told about the things you made Sarah do under the guise of showmanship. At any rate, I need no business partner, associate, or advisor. I merely asked if you knew her whereabouts. Furthermore, I'm here in the interest of science.

Culvier. No injury intended Doctor. However, I am certain your interest in Sarah Bartman holds a monetary value.

[Passerby looks into house and runs off yelling.]

Passerby. Sarah Bartman is dead. Sarah Bartman is dead!

[Doctor and Culvier stare at each other in surprise. Then push and shove trying to get to her first.]

Doctor. Out of my way. I need to examine her body.

Culvier. You are out of your element here, Doctor.

(Shepherd appears enraged in the doorway. Both men jump in shock.)

Shepherd. Her body is not yet cold and you vultures are here to pick her bones!

Culvier. My God, it is your man-servant.

Doctor. Well, the prodigal returns. **(Pause)**
Shepherd, step aside I have business here.

**Shepherd. (Crosses his arms defiantly blocking
the doorway.)** You destroyed her in life. You will not
defile her in death.

Doctor. I did no such thing. Sarah made her own
decisions. They were just bad ones. Now, I intend to
examine the body then give her a proper burial.

Shepherd. Your false words hold no merit with
anyone; least of all me. Now go about your way, sir.

Doctor. I shall not. How dare you take such a tone
with me? I am still your master. You ran away from
my supervision to become a fugitive and a vagabond.
You shall pay for your insolence. **(Raises his cane)** I
shall beat you like your former master use to.

Shepherd. Well, step forward Doctor so that I may
rid the world of your filth. **(Steps from doorway.
Pulls out a gun and aims it steadily at the
Doctor.)**

Culvier. Good lord, man. Your Negro has a firearm.
I know times are changing but I don't think it's legal
for Negroes to own firearms. **(Runs off yelling)**
Help...Help...

[Enter Prostitute]

Prostitute. A doctor is on the way. How is... **(She sees Sarah dead and kneels down in the doorway crying.)**

Doctor. Shepherd do you really think the specter of death frightens me? I knew this day would come. But I did not imagine it would come by such a dark hand. You shall meet with a firing squad before the week is done.

Prostitute. Dear sir, you are the Shepherd Sarah always spoke of? Then you must know she would not want you to end your life this way.

Shepherd. You know nothing of this monster.

Doctor. I am the monster who fed you, clothed you, and educated you. Your mother abandoned you. I'm the only father you know.

Shepherd. Cease your blasphemy monster. **(Puts gun to Doctor's head.)**

Doctor. **(Crouching)** Go on then, kill me. I shall be with Christ this day.

Shepherd. You shall soon see.

Prostitute. Shepherd, please kind sir, I beg you. Sarah would not want this for you.

[Whistle blows and voice yells "over there."]

Doctor. (Shivering) I'm ready to die now! **(Urinates in his pants)**

Shepherd. (Leans forward and looks at the Doctor's wet pants.) Indeed. **(He mashes the Doctor's face and he falls to the ground cowering. Shepherd walks back over to Sarah's body.)** Goodnight Sarah, my love. Now you are truly free. **(Exits.) (Curtain.)**

Act IV

Scene: [Doctor alone on stage with body parts on display]

Doctor. Step right up ladies and gentlemen. Behold the disembodied remains of the freak known across all Europe as the 'Hottentot Venus' Sarah Bartman. Do not look upon me like that, sir. I assure you that I did not kill her. I merely dissected and preserved her peculiar body for your viewing pleasure. Before her untimely death, Sarah granted me permission via this signed contract, to secure her remains and do what was best for the scientific community.

 So, for a small fee I shall allow you to gaze upon her freakish remains before they're placed within the confines of one of England's most prestigious museums. **(Points to man in audience)** You sir, don't be shy, step forward. You ma'am, come have a look see. In case you are wondering, I have no conscience. Therefore I have no shame. And judging from the money I've made, neither...do...you!

[Close Curtain]

The End.

Also by Julius Kane:

Innocence and Necessity

Accusation and Denial

Contact: juliuskane@ymail.com

The Strange Fruits of Sarah Bartman by Julius Kane